# THE RENEGADES

## BOOK ONE: RENEGADES RISE

THEGLASSESCOMEOFF

First edition 2016
PRINTED BY BLURB
www.theglassescomeoff.com

[1. Fantasy—Fiction.   2. Adventure—Fiction.]
Text set in EB Garamond
Cover Illustration by Audra Balion
Interior Formatted by IIDesigns, www.iibookdesigns.com

ALSO BY BRIAN JAMES HILDEBRAND

*One Spell*

Defy The World, Do What's Right!

Brian Hildebrand

## ACKNOWLEDGEMENTS

To F. David Schultz, Nicole Zalesak, Adam Formanek, Kristy Bieber, and Rissa Weitzel for being beta readers for this book. To Audra Balion, Cover artist, and another of the beta readers. To Lindsay McDonald of IIDesigns, for being a patient, understanding editor.

And to my tabletop roleplaying group, the Irregulars, who gave me the inspiration for this series when we started a superhero campaign: Colin Pitman, Corey Schultz, Sean Carr, Amanda Carr, and Amy Pitman (who was also a beta reader).

## DEDICATION

To everyone who knows that success requires you to be more afraid of not trying than you are of failing, and to everyone who will be inspired by those words.

# ❶

## CLAIRE
### THE SPARROW

My name is Claire O'Sheen, the Sparrow. I'm a superhero. Though not the kind that most are familiar with. I'm not with the Hero Society. I was, once. But that was before everything changed.

It all started on the day I was kidnapped. I had been walking to school, ready to enjoy what was seeming like an ordinary day for a change, when they showed up. A half dozen supervillains, the Thugs, popped out of nowhere, grabbed me, and shoved me in a van.

They put me in a warehouse. I was tied down to a chair, blindfolded, and listened as one of the world's most ruthless gangs of criminals decided my fate. I heard them talking and debating. Even when they whispered, I caught every word. I should have been scared. I should have been angry, furious at the world for doing that to me, for letting me get kidnapped. But I wasn't. Instead, I actually had to hold back the hugest smile.

Back then, I was Osprey, sidekick of founding Hero Society Member Rush, and the daughter of founding member Eagle. And all I could think as I was tied to that chair was that taking down the Thugs all by myself would earn me the right to stop being a sidekick and become a full-fledged member of the Society.

It felt like the world was handing my full hero membership to me on a silver platter. The Thugs had literally kidnapped me without any clue of who I really was. It was almost too good to be true.

My face stung after one of them slapped me. The blindfold they had put on me was ripped off as one of them said, "Who's next?"

I surveyed the room. The Thugs' membership had changed over the years; I wasn't too sure who all I was dealing with. A glance around the room showed me the Thugs had gone through some recruitment since the last time I helped fight them. There was Jimmy-Two-Selves standing in the corner, his rainbow outfit a painful eyesore even more than the cheesy goggles he wore as a mask. To my surprise there was only one of him. I shuddered as I noticed Marksman, wearing his cliché poacher outfit. I'd tussled with him in my sidekick days. Marksman may have no powers, but he's still the last Thug I'd want to fight. I also spotted Regurg, a bit of a bulge to him and a sickly purple outfit that made people who looked at it want to lose their lunch. Fitting, considering his powers, since he could eat anything and remake his body into any substance still in his stomach. And of course, Puppeteer, painfully lazy from all the reports I've read, but just one touch and he could make you do whatever he wanted for a couple minutes. I was surprised he hadn't used his powers on me. But reports on him said that people he tried to control slowly built up an immunity, so maybe he wasn't going to waste time controlling me if he didn't need to.

The other three were new recruits. They all looked pretty young to me, not that I'm old at the charming age of sixteen. One was in a pale blue outfit with cloud and lightning bolt patterns. Weather powers, I guessed. It never made sense to me that villains would wear costumes that reveal their powers. Wear a suit of flames if you use water—that brief instant of confusion could mean the difference between victory and defeat.

The other two were rather plain. A very tall, built man in a greyish-brown spandex number and a girl dressed all in grey.

I couldn't help but wonder which of the Thugs was the new leader of their little gang—their original leader, Blaster, had been arrested by the Hero Society a month ago. My money was on Jimmy-Two Selves; he'd been with the Thugs the longest.

Weather patterns boy ran his hand along my cheek and purred, "Ain't she a beauty, boys? Hair's a little short, but she wears it so nicely."

I subtly struggled with my restraints as I watched the room. The restraints were not as tight as they thought they were, and while they'd been busy chattering away, I'd slipped a scalpel I carry for just these occasions out of my wrist sheath.

The brown-suited man glared at weather patterns. "Leave her alone, Climate. You have her mom's number. Call for the ransom so we can get out of here."

"Patience, Geo," Climate responded with a smile, "I'm the boss. And the boss wants to have a little fun with her."

I masked my surprise. The new guy looked like he was barely my age, and yet he was the leader of the Thugs? It was just plain weird.

"Fun? With the girl who has won martial arts competitions?" Jimmy Two-Selves tossed in.

"Every other girl who goes to that preppy douche school gets driven to school with guards and a limo. She's the only one who walks. Besides, I like my girls a little spunky."

"This goes against everything the Thugs stand for, Climate, and you know it. Blaster's rules were always that we never hurt innocent people. We rob, we take money, but we never hurt anyone," Geo cut in angrily.

"And is Mr. Zach 'Blaster' O'Brien around to say a thing?" Climate asked, his voice pouty and condescending. He didn't wait for anyone to answer before shouting gleefully, "I don't think so!"

Climate slapped me again.

Before I could make him pay for that, Geo did it for me. The ground split open and a mass of earth shot at Climate. Climate shot a bolt of lightning at it, and the chunk of dirt exploded harmlessly into powder.

"Do that again, and I'll kill you, Ethan," Climate responded as he took off his mask.

I knew my time to act had been cut short. Everyone knows that if your captors show their faces, they don't plan to let you live. Even if they were trying to get a ransom from my mom, they didn't plan to hand me over. Climate didn't seem inclined to, anyway.

I tried to think of an escape plan. But something nagged at the back of my head. Climate had called Geo Ethan. I knew that was important.

And then it hit me. Ethan was the son of two of the original Thugs, Strongman and Dynamite. Those two had been killed by the Hero Society over a year ago in the war against the Villains Coalition.

The other Thugs looked a bit afraid as Climate stepped up to me and said, "You're a pretty smart girl, aren't you, Miss Claire O'Sheen. Smart, and skilled, and...kind of pretty."

He actually flirted with me. It was downright hilarious. Unfortunately, I couldn't contain myself. A slight giggle escaped.

"You're laughing?" Climate snapped, in utter shock. "Tied up, in a room with some of the most terrifying villains in the world, and you're laughing? Well, we can do something about that, don't you agree, Ethan?"

Ethan said nothing, but I could see the look on his face. It was the look you give someone that you want to kill.

"You know, Ethan," Climate continued, "you've been with the gang for a pretty short amount of time. I don't think you've really earned your Thug stripes yet."

"And you have?" Geo replied, anger dripping from his voice.

"Oh, I'm as bad as they come. Sure, I'm new on the scene, but I'm hot! I mean, I'm already leader of the Thugs. And as leader, I think it's important to make sure I know where your loyalties lie. Kill the girl."

I'd sliced away at my bonds while the two new guys to the club squabbled.

I tore my bonds and leapt from the seat, taking a swing at the man who had just been ordered to kill me. Before anyone could respond, I flipped around and spun a kick straight into Climate's chest.

Climate seemed more surprised than hurt as he shouted, "Get her!"

There were too many of them, and only one of me. Every move I made needed to count. I tossed my scalpel at Puppeteer and embedded it in his chest. Not that the blade was long enough to do any permanent damage, but Puppeteer was too much of a coward to do anything after he was hurt.

Climate shot a bolt of lightning at me, but before it could collide, a pillar of earth shot up and blocked the blow, grounding the lightning.

"What are you doing?" Climate shouted.

Geo said nothing as the ground around us ruptured and started to shake. With all of the shaking, I started to worry. I had no idea how strong Geo was. For all I knew, he could create an earthquake.

Chunks of earth and bits of dirt and dust flew around the room; it was like fighting in a sandstorm. I shouldn't have been able to see at all.

But see, I could. Jimmy Two-Selves and Marksman left the fight. Regurg wasn't having much of a problem, his body had turned to solid steel and he was coming at me. But I knew exactly what to do to deal with Regurg.

I tried to shout, give Geo some instructions, but nothing came out. A quick glance showed me that the girl in grey had glowing eyes. I wasn't too sure what she could do, but it looked like sound manipulation of some kind.

I raced at Regurg, my right fist ready. I wasn't stupid enough to punch solid steel, but I was ready for him. As my closed fist connected with his body, I activated my ring, and a surge of electricity shot through his body, stunning him.

Regurg then did what he named himself for, and steel balls, table pieces, and more came surging out of his mouth.

Puppeteer, who had been quiet most of the time, shouted as he saw what happened.

"That...that's an electro-ring. Eagle uses one, and so does the sidekick Osprey! Guys, we have to run!"

"Why, 'cause we captured a sidekick? I'd say this is the perfect opportunity to show the world how the new and improved Thugs operate," Climate shouted. He shot a bolt of lightning in my direction, but with all the dirt in the air, his aim was way off. He started to create some hail to pelt me with, but with all of the dust and dirt, it was just adding to the chaos.

"If she's a sidekick, then we are gonna have the Society itself down our necks any second now."

Climate glared. "Don't let her escape!"

Geo turned to me, pulling my face around to look at his. He wasn't speaking out loud, but I think he was counting on me being able to read lips. He was right, I could. "Trust me, and hold your breath."

The ground swallowed up both of us as Geo pulled me in close to him. It was a very weird feeling, the very earth itself was pushing us around.

It lasted about thirty seconds, and then we were outside, and free.

I ripped myself away from Geo, ready to fight him. He was a Thug. And I was a sidekick. I needed to take him down, even if he had helped me.

He looked at me with a combination of surprise and outrage. "I saved your life, and you're going to attack me?"

"Saving my life doesn't give you a pass for all the crimes you've committed."

Angry, he dove back underground with his powers and was gone before I could do a single thing to stop him.

But he couldn't hide from me. I knew his name. I wasn't going to need anything else to find him and use him to take down all of the Thugs. I was sure it was going to be a great day. If only I'd known what was coming.

# ETHAN
## GEO

You might think that when your life is officially screwed, completely over, that the first thing you would do is give up. It's not. You look for any scrap, any excuse, to hang on. And for me, that was my family.

I cursed myself as I ran home.

I'd fought against Climate, Steven. I'd betrayed the Thugs. I had to get home, pack, and get ready to leave. Get my family out of the city.

I made a burrow and changed back into my civilian clothes before surfacing in the backyard. The house was still intact as I ran in the backdoor.

No one else was home. Which was good, though something of a miracle. Julie and I try to wrangle our five younger siblings every morning and make sure they get to school at all, let alone on time, and tend to have some mixed success with that. But even bothering to try and get them to school is more than Mom and Dad ever did.

I wasn't the best father-figure in the world, not by a long shot. But when your parents were among the worst in the world, it's not hard to do a better job than they did.

I ran upstairs to my closet and grabbed the three duffle bags I had stashed. Full to the brim. Emergency clothes, toothbrushes, toothpaste, and all the other stuff that the kids would need if we needed to leave town on a moment's notice.

I ran to Whitney's room and grabbed Mr. Fuzzlybies, her stuffed lion. No chance she would leave the city without it.

As I stuffed Mr. Fuzzlybies into a bag, the phone rang. I hesitated to answer it, especially when I saw who it was on the other end.

"James," I said, referring to Jimmy-Two-Selves by his real name.

"Ethan, what you did was pretty stupid."

"You think I don't know that?"

"Look, Melissa, Colin, and I are going to try and smooth things over. Convince Steven that he pushed things too far and that he needs to forgive you or he'll lose half the gang."

That might be the way to go. The easier way. But did I really want to? Did I really want to be a part of the Thugs?

Like I needed to ask myself that question. The answer was and always had been no. I had never wanted to join the Thugs.

There weren't many options as a nineteen-year-old high-school dropout struggling to raise six kids aged from four to sixteen though. The Thugs were the only way to get the kind of money I needed to raise them. But I knew I couldn't stay if it meant following Steven's lead.

"Thanks, James. But I can't come back. I've never been a good fit, even before psychopath Steven. You should get Melissa out of there. That's what I'm gonna do. Grab my brothers and sisters and get the heck out of town. Steven won't get better, you know that."

I could feel James's hesitation as he said, "The Thugs stood for something, we can't just run away from that."

"Maybe you can't, but I can."

"I'm sorry to see you go," James replied, "send me the new address after you move, I'll make sure the kids get their Christmas gifts from Mel and me."

"Thanks," I said, "I will."

I was lying. For a criminal, James may not have been the worst person in the world, but there was still no way I was telling any member of the gang where I was going.

I started to phone the schools. First up, Julie.

"Hello," I said to the secretary after she picked up, "This is Ethan Johnson. I'm afraid there has been some family trouble, may I please talk to Julie?"

It didn't take long for Julie to call me back. "What's the emergency, bro?" Julie asked.

"I quit."

I heard Julie gasp on the other end. "Steven pushed the line again?"

"Yeah," I said, trying to hold back my tears, "We kidnapped someone...and then...." I struggled to get the words out, "Steven told me to kill her."

"You have the bags packed?" Julie asked, her voice telling me I had her complete support.

"Yes."

"I'll go and pick up Whitney, Nate, Brad, and Tiffany. Can you go get Mike and take the bags with you? I'll meet you at his school."

"Sure thing." I grabbed the bags.

"Good, I'll see you in half an hour, an hour tops."

"See you." I hung up the phone, grabbed the duffle bags, and ran to Mike's school. It was only a couple of blocks away. I could get there fast enough that calling was a waste of time.

I walked inside, looking for the main office so that they could call down Mike for me.

"Hello," I greeted the secretary.

"May I help you?" she asked.

"I'm Mike Johnson's older brother. There's been a family emergency and I need to take him out of class."

She looked at me skeptically. I got that look any time I dealt with anyone who knew who we were. The deaths of my parents had been public news so everyone knew that we were the children of supervillains. And that was a sure-fire way to get bullied in school, surprisingly enough, then receive no sympathy from the teachers. I couldn't even get a job because of my parents' reputation. We were treated like criminals just because our parents were.

The secretary looked through her records and found the details of Mike's classroom. She called down. "Hello, I have someone to see Mike Johnson." She nodded and answered "okay" into the phone a half dozen times before hanging up and getting back to me. "It would appear that Mike is not here. Do you know where he might be?"

"If I did, I'd be there, not here," I said, angrier than I intended to be, panic overriding everything else.

"There's no need for that tone," the secretary said in a very huffy voice. I could see the principal and vice principal in their offices looking out at me now. The vice principal was a big man, not as big as I am, but pretty close. The principal was on the phone. Wouldn't surprise me if he was calling 911. Not the first time someone jumped to that conclusion about members of my family.

"You're right," I said, trying to relax, and probably failing, "I just...I need to know where he is. It's really important."

"I'm sure it is..." the secretary replied, clearly thinking I had some kind of ulterior motive.

"Please," I started lying, "I need help finding him. The Thugs...they think that my parents have some money stashed away, and they're going to hurt my family if I don't give it to them. I need to get them somewhere safe."

I could hear the principal, no longer whispering into the phone, "Forget what I just said. We have reason to believe that the Thugs themselves are coming after one of our students, the son of one of their former members. Yes, one of Strongman and Dynamite's kids. He's gone missing already."

He paused for a moment, listening, then met my eye. "Your other siblings?"

"I called Julie, she's driving to the elementary school to get them."

"The elder sister is headed to their elementary school. Yes, I agree, it would be best if they were taken into police custody, for their own safety."

I sat down for a moment. Trying to process everything and figure out where Mike would go.

"If the Thugs might show up here, then we need to do something to be ready for them. You'll be safer here, if you want to stay."

"Mike's missing. I need to be out looking for him."

I raced out of the building, one thought burning in my mind: where was Mike?

# CLAIRE

## THE SPARROW

"What were you thinking?" my mother shouted at me.

"Survive," I snapped. I'd been kidnapped, I'd fought the hardest I'd ever fought in my entire life, to escape. Seven supervillains alone, and here I was alive. No sidekick had ever done that before.

But that didn't matter to my mom.

A video of the fight had made its way online. One of the Thugs must have uploaded it.

In less time than you'd think possible, people commenting online had pointed out that the ring I used was an electro-ring. The weapon that The Eagle was famous for using. It didn't take long for someone to comment that Rush had a sidekick named Osprey who was using Eagle tech.

But that wasn't the worst part. Someone online commented that they recognized me, Claire O'Sheen.

They proved it by comparing stills of the video to sports articles about my martial arts and gymnastics awards.

All in all, it only took the tabloids two hours to begin phoning my mom, Brenda O'Sheen, asking whether or not she was The Eagle, founding member of the Hero Society.

After almost fifteen years of successfully staying in the shadows, the secret identity of one of the original members of the Hero Society had become public knowledge.

And the Hero Society decided it was my fault.

"The world figured out who I am, Claire. You can't just shrug that off so easily."

"I'm not shrugging anything off, Mom," I replied angrily. "They were going to kill me. I made sure they didn't."

"What is Society rule number 1?" my mom asked. As if I hadn't had the rules completely memorized for the last ten years of my life.

"'The identities of all members remain a secret; you die before you give up a Hero's identity, even your own,'" I quoted.

"And what did you do? You used a weapon distinctly associated with both of our secret identities."

"You know, most mothers would be happy that their daughter was alive."

My mother waved her hand in the air as if to dismiss my comments. "You've been able to handle yourself in a fight since you were ten years old. Don't act like I should have been worried about you."

I hated admitting she was right, but she was. She didn't have to worry about me.

"Okay, I messed up while trying to take down some of the most well-known criminals around. It happens."

"Not on this scale," she said, "now I have to go out to the world and publicly acknowledge that I am, indeed, The Eagle."

"Why not just erase the video or something?"

"Too many people have seen it. Accursed internet. It's impossible for anyone to keep a secret anymore."

I slumped into my chair. Nothing like this had ever happened before, and I was honestly scared of what it meant. "So, what happens now?" I asked.

"I've talked with all of the Society members that I could get a hold of," Mom said, "And I'm sorry to say that I agree with them, Claire."

"Mom...what did you agree to?" To say I was anything less than terrified would be a lie. I'd seen people locked up for life just for revealing the secret identity of any hero, let alone a Hero Society leader.

"Claire, sweetie...." The red lights in my head were blaring. For my mom to call me sweetie, something very bad was about to happen. "The Hero Society and I have decided that you are to cease being a sidekick or hero, immediately and indefinitely. You will forfeit your costume and all equipment to me and continue your life as an ordinary citizen."

I felt like someone had punctured the very balloon of all my dreams. I'd wanted to be a hero since forever. It was the only thing I had ever wanted to do. Mastering gymnastics, martial arts, chemistry, physics, and machinery. I'd been working hard my entire life to take my place in the Hero Society's core membership.

I slammed my fists down on the table, and I'm pretty sure I cracked it. Mom didn't look too happy about that.

"Claire...we didn't come to this decision easily. But you should have known better. This isn't some little mistake that will just go away. This is going to affect you for the rest of your life. Every single one of our friends is going to immediately fall under suspicion as being another hero. We can't expose any of them, that will put them and everyone they care about at risk. So no more shopping trips with Jillian, I'm afraid. No more coffee with Sarah for me. No more Hero Society dinners at our house. They're all done."

"I get it. Can I go now? I still have homework to do, unless getting high marks in school is acting too much like a sidekick for you."

I stormed off to my bedroom. Banned from being a sidekick? I couldn't believe she would do that to me. I didn't know what to do. Didn't know what to think. I wasn't going to be all pouty and cry about it though. That's not me.

I couldn't ignore my hero ban though. I could still remember the screams from when Aviator broke his ban only to get arrested by the Society.

But then—Black Death had accidentally killed dozens of people before he gained control of his powers, and his hard work and vital importance in taking down one of the Society's most-wanted villains earned him not just a reprieve, but elevation to one of the Society's leaders.

My ban wasn't permanent. Not if I could do something big enough to prove that I was more than one mistake.

And I had just the plan.

I hopped on my computer to do some research and was bombarded by everyone trying to talk to me about what had happened.

I had messages from just about everyone in my classes, and a few hundred people who weren't. Most of them were making fun of me, how I must be an incredible screw-up, to be the first person in history to accidentally reveal a Hero's secret identity.

I glanced down at the electro-ring still on my finger and then tossed it in the trash. Not like I was going to need it anymore.

Eventually, I ignored the messages to focus on what I needed to find. Ethan was the son of Jake and Sally Johnson: Strongman and Dynamite. I knew that if I could find where he lived, I could capture him and make him lead me to the rest of the Thugs. Taking down the Thugs had to get me reinstated as a sidekick, if not made into a full-fledged Hero. The Thugs had been a gang of supervillains almost as long as superpowers had existed. If taking them down didn't do the trick, then the Society was expecting the impossible. I typed in "Ethan Johnson" "Strongman" and "Dynamite" into a search engine and hoped for the best.

I went over to my closet, and grabbed out a trio of old shoe boxes. I'd been keeping a few items in there. Some knock-out gas pellets, an icy freezing pellet. A cloak designed to catch the wind and become solid, like wings, essentially working as a hang glider; impact gloves designed with some handy mechanical engineering to extend forward at an intense speed after a punch, adding extra oomph to every hit. All my own tech, made it myself, to set me apart from my mom one day. She didn't know about any of it. There was a costume in the box too. More Kevlar based, darker. Browns and Greys.

I put the suit on underneath my clothes—now was not the time to go hopping about in a hero costume—and I headed out the door. I'd found where he lived. It was time I paid Geo a little visit.

# ④

# VALERIE
## STELLAR

I awoke to yet another day in paradise, locked in a twelve-by-twelve-foot Hero Society jail cell. I tossed my nose ring and earrings on; never could sleep while wearing them. Gave my hair a quick rinse and looked at my tattoos. I took a moment to brush my hair, out of boredom more than anything. I even threw on some lipstick, because I may not be allowed a computer or a TV, and books are carefully regulated, but letting me have cosmetics in prison wasn't a problem. I spent an hour or two every morning making myself look nice. Not like I had anywhere to go, or anyone worth looking good for, but the routine helped kill time every day and that was reason enough.

I could feel Dorian pacing in the cell above my own.

There was the faintest touch of a shadow sparkling in the corner of my cell, like a floating penny of darkness. I walked over to it. "Dorian, what do you want?" I asked into the void, knowing full well that Dorian could hear me through it.

It still amazed me that he could pull this off. These prison cells were designed to neutralize powers, or at the very least, contain and redirect them so that we couldn't use them. But leave it to Dorian, former crime boss and leader of the Villains Coalition, to find a way around even that.

Not that he'd been able to use it to escape, he still couldn't manage to make anything bigger than an inch or two long.

"Today is the day, Valerie. I hope that you will be joining the rest of us."

The day. Dorian had been talking about it for as long as I'd been there. Which is to say, non-freakin'-stop for three months.

"You've been talking about escaping this place since before I arrived," I said, "What's so special about today?"

"I've always been able to escape, Valerie. What's so special, is that now I have every single prisoner willing to side with me when I escape."

"Except for me," I finished. "And really, all of them? At least a quarter of the people in here are wannabe superheroes only imprisoned for violating Hero Society law or refusing to sign up after becoming a hero."

"Revenge is a strong motivator. I would have thought that you would want revenge more than anyone. You weren't even trying to be a hero or a villain, and they arrested you anyway."

"Don't remind me," I replied.

It was true though, I had gotten pretty much the worst prize that anyone in the world could get from the Hero Society.

Cliff notes version? I was a teenage prodigy. Still am, I guess, since I'm only seventeen. I invented some nanotechnology that was in a league of its own. I hadn't done anything with my tech, just shown the world that it existed, that I could build it. And it was so powerful that the Society feared me. Three years ago, they literally came to my doorstep and told me that I had to sign over my nanotechnology to a science firm they approved of or my tech would be labelled a threat to global security and I would be locked away.

I agreed, and worked for their science firm. Three years of being one of the best paid scientists in the world, and all it cost was any level of privacy.

They had told me that with a brain like mine that I needed bodyguards, but it felt more like having a constant babysitter. I wasn't allowed to go anywhere without a bodyguard present. And I mean anywhere. One of my guards was always female so that I wouldn't have to go to the bathroom alone. All to make sure my tech never fell into the wrong hands.

Which were apparently my own. Because after I started designing plans to use the nanotech to create a battle suit similar to the one used by Steel Soldier of the Hero Society, they asked me if I was planning on using the suit to become a hero.

I said no, these plans were to help military forces and such by giving all soldiers the capacity to fight against powered people.

The Hero Society didn't like that. Cause those hypocrites hate the idea of any kind of power being mass-produced and available to the world. They pulled me off the project. They stopped me from working on my own invention.

Well, they tried to. I continued doing the research on my own. Stole back my old files.

Within an hour of doing so I found myself arrested as a threat to global security and thrown in a Hero Society jail cell. All because I wanted to be a scientist, not a hero.

Dorian was right. If anyone had a just reason to hate the Hero Society, it was me.

But that didn't mean I was okay with becoming a villain. I just wanted a way out of the cell, a way to have a life again, when mine was taken away for no good reason.

"What do you need from me, Dorian?" I asked.

"Need? I need nothing," Dorian said, in that confident voice of his that was so easy to believe if you didn't know the facts.

"Please. I don't even have any powers. I'm essentially useless in a fight. And yet you feel the need to convince me to join you when you could have some mind controller just force me to follow suit."

I could feel Dorian's impatience growing, even though his silky but strong voice was attempting to hide it. "You were able to hack into the files of a laboratory that had Society-level security. Even if they were able to trace it back to you within an hour, the mere fact that you got in is impressive. It's never been done before. Your brain may be the most valuable thing in these cells."

I almost smiled. Sometimes I like a bit of flattery. "Okay...what's in it for me?"

"Get me Society secrets, and I will get your tech back. I have a bit of an army at my disposal."

I wanted my tech back. But siding with Dorian was not a decision I could make lightly. Dorian had been the leader of the Villains Coalition before his arrest. There had literally been thousands of villains following his every command. Siding with him would make me a villain for the rest of my life.

After what felt like an eternity of debate, I came to a decision. Better to be free and wanted, than an innocent prisoner. "Dorian," I said, "You have a deal."

"Then let's begin," Dorian replied.

Suddenly, all of the doors were open. All of our cells, with their force field and electric barrier locks, were opened. Not that it did anything for me, six stories up and no stairs. Then Dorian appeared in my cell, a half-dozen other villains alongside him. I recognized a couple, Monster and Blaster, both leading members of the Villains Coalition. There were a couple others that I wasn't as familiar with. An elderly woman who didn't look like she was a threat at all, a man whose costume had enough gun and sword holsters on him to double as a pawn shop, and a woman with a third eye tattooed on her forehead, like members of the Psychic sisterhood.

Dorian gestured to me. "Do move quickly, please."

I stepped into Dorian's darkmatter portal, a weird thing that looks like you're staring out into space, full of white star flecks against an infinite blackness.

Stepping out into a hallway of Society headquarters, I witnessed a dozen heroes trying to stop us, led by Steel Soldier herself. There was an enormous locked door beside us, and an access panel to the right of it.

"Cover me," I said as I ran to the door and began working on unlocking it.

Dorian bellowed at the others, "You heard her. Make sure she gets a little privacy."

Dorian tossed one of his darkmatter orbs at Steel Soldier. Steel Soldier dodged the blow, but was immediately struck by a shot from Blaster's arms. A blast that almost hit Monster in the process.

"Watch where you're shooting!" Monster shouted.

"Sorry, without my control gauntlets my blasts have always been a bit erratic."

"Idiots and amateurs," the elderly woman in the group said. Suddenly, everything started moving much slower around us.

"What just..." Dorian asked.

"I slowed down time. You idiots appeared to need the help," the elderly woman said as a literal demon appeared in front of her, standing on cloven hooves with large black wings and enormous horns on its head. It looked kind of cheesy. But there was nothing cheesy about it grabbing two heroes and throwing them through a wall a hundred feet away.

I did my best to ignore all of this and focus on unlocking the door. Not that it was that hard. For all the importance they put behind them, Society locks are surprisingly easy to open. I had disabled all of their traps, unlocked the door, and was about to walk right on through. And then I was pushed back as I came into contact with...something.

But I'd disabled absolutely everything on the computer. So it wasn't tech.

I bit my tongue to stop from screaming in frustration as I realized that the room was also protected by magic. I hate magic.

"Hey, magic lady!" I shouted over the noise. "I got the locks and codes down, but it looks like there's a magic barrier still in the way. Think you can get rid of it?"

"Please, infant, the day that a member of the Society surpasses my capacities in magic is the day that magic ceases to exist."

She and I were not going to get along, I could already tell.

I stepped out of her way as she used her magic.

"Is it gone?" I asked.

"Only one way to find out," she said, and with a thrust of magic, tossed me into the room.

I didn't hit anything, so I guess it was okay. I went to quick work on the panel on the other side and shouted, "Get in here, now!"

They got the message, and all dove to get into the room with me as I sealed the door behind us. I could hear the heroes slamming against it on the other side and trying to open it. But the door was strong. It took brains, not brawn, to get through it; and way too many heroes, and villains, use the latter not the former.

"Good work, Valerie," Dorian said as he looked around the room, "we're actually in their vault. All the items they confiscated should be here."

"Little Miss Brains wouldn't have gotten us anywhere if my magic hadn't countered their magic," the elderly woman huffed.

"And if you were more modest about it," Dorian retorted, "I'd say 'Good work, Mother Time' too."

I hid my smirk by turning back to the computer. "Okay, I've got an inventory list here, but can't take it with me."

Mother Time sighed and was about to cast a spell when weapon holster man, speaking up for what was definitely his first time, said, "Are you that arrogant—or that stupid? Magic and tech don't mix!"

"Sure they do," Dorian replied, "Just not easily. I've seen it."

"Now this is what I need," the man ready to carry an arsenal said as he opened one of the lockers and pulled out swords, guns, and knives, and began to sheath them all.

"Feeling better Weaponize?" Dorian asked.

"Much," Weaponize responded as he shoved a clip into a semi-automatic pistol.

I ignored them. "Blaster, your control gauntlets are in Aisle F, row 8. As for other stuff, they apparently keep the best stuff in a vault in the centre of the room."

"To their vault," Dorian ordered.

We ran down the hallway to the vault. I wished Dorian could just teleport us there, but it would seem he couldn't go anywhere he hadn't been before. He could get us all out of here whenever he wanted. But he wanted something more before we left.

As we made it to the vault, I heard the sound of the door breaking behind us. A human-sized hole had been punched through it. And flying at us from that hole was Paragon herself.

All of the others were ready to take her, but even I could know how tense they felt. Paragon was undisputedly the most powerful member of the Society, arguably stronger than all of the others combined.

I opened the vault and looked inside. Two items. That was it. A book and a gun.

Dorian looked at the gun, it was of an alien design of some kind. It looked like a large rifle, but was glowing from what I assume was the end the shot fired from. It didn't have a single hole for a bullet or laser, but instead had a curved vent at the front which it appeared to fire from. He smiled at it and said, "That's...that's one of the guns that caused the Eclipse!"

I was starting to regret helping Dorian in that moment. If this was an eclipse gun, then it might be able to do what the eclipse did, and give people superpowers.

But it was not the most valuable thing in the room, according to some. The deep violet book with its huge inlaid ruby and gold trim had certainly gathered the attention of the old nutcase.

"The Book of Darkness!" Mother Time shouted as she reached in and grabbed the book, "It's mine. It's finally mine!"

Dorian grabbed the gun and opened one of his darkmatter portals. I stepped through it just as Paragon flew in and almost took my head off.

We had escaped, and with hundreds of supervillains running around in Society headquarters, they weren't going to be chasing us anytime soon. A clean getaway.

# 5

## XAPHAN

The hellfire was burning brightly this morning. The screams of tortured souls filled the air. But I had grown numb to such sounds millennia ago. I just made the fire, and kept it burning. The sounds of torture were the department of another.

"Hey, Xaphan," Shax yelled, "message for you."

"Thank you, Shax," I replied, "I will take it in my office."

"Sure thing. We on for the backgammon tournament tonight?"

"Play against you? I think not."

"Suit yourself, hot stuff."

I ignored Shax's comment. Some human slang makes it down to the underworld, alongside the worst of humanity that it comes with. Shax believed it was funny, referring to me as hot considering my occupation as keeper of the hellfire. Though with my body constantly grimy and covered in soot from my time with the hellfire, the meaning of 'hot stuff' as 'an attractive person' would be inaccurate. Shax would also claim it was because I looked feminine. From what I recall, I suppose it would be accurate to say I more closely resemble a human female than a human male. Masculinity and femininity do not protrude as distinctly among us as they do among humans. I try not to waste my time thinking on such trivialities.

Arriving in my office, I witnessed the letter upon my desk. Unopened, with the seal of Lucifer upon it. For Lucifer to be sending me a message, something important must be happening.

I opened the letter with care, and read Lucifer's words. Short, and to the point.

*Xaphan, there is a matter about which I wish to speak with you promptly. Find someone to take over for you and report to me immediately.*

I folded the letter and placed it into my pocket. Then I walked out of my office. I headed for Vapula's laboratory. I could ask a hundred different Fallen to take over the hellfire duties for me and they would all be happy and willing. And they would all mess it up. Overheating the entire Underworld in their attempts to make it clear that they do not go easy on those being punished. They think that being cruel is the key to obtaining more power in the Underworld. They do not understand Lucifer at all.

I knocked upon the entry to Vapula's lab and noticed that Vapula was presently engaged in some experiment.

"I hope I am not interrupting," I said.

"I am almost done," Vapula replied. "May I have a minute to finish this, please?"

"Provided you actually mean a minute instead of the day you made me wait last time, then yes."

Vapula nodded, and I prepared to wait for a month. Vapula was brilliant, but to get Vapula to do anything other than experiments was nigh impossible.

Vapula did actually finish the task quickly and efficiently, much to my surprise.

"How can I help you, Xaphan?"

"I need you to take over the hellfires today."

"You could not find anyone else?"

"You know exactly what happened the last time someone other than you took over from me for a day."

"We ran out of hellfire because someone became overzealous."

"Correct. Which is why it needs to be you."

"Why do you need to take the day off?" Vapula asked.

I pulled out the letter and showed Vapula the seal. "A meeting with Lucifer."

That caught Vapula's attention. Vapula's wings shuddered at the thought of a meeting with Lucifer. "Meeting Lucifer...that is a good reason. Anything I should know before you go? Any changes since last time?"

"Only one," I said, "torture on Hercules is to be diminished. Lucifer's orders. Hercules needs to believe he is not important enough to warrant more torture than anyone else."

"Okay. Come back in one piece so that I don't have to keep your job."

"Don't worry. I will."

I left Vapula's laboratory and headed straight to Lucifer's chambers. The guards on duty were quick to let me past as I headed for Lucifer's office rather than the throne room. Most would believe Lucifer stays in the ornate throne room when not busy with other tasks. They fail to realize that Lucifer is far safer in his office, and fail to realize how important safety is when one faces several attempted assassinations every week.

Lucifer stood as I entered the room. Blond hair, blue eyes, and fair skin. Even in the depths of the underworld, Lucifer maintained a classy and impeccable look.

Lucifer smiled upon noticing me.

"Xaphan, it has been far too long. How are you?"

"As well as can be expected."

"Anything new?"

"You need not waste time on civility with me, Lucifer. I would prefer you did not, if being so honest is not disrespectful."

Lucifer's smile grew wider, and with a quick gesture for me to take a seat, Lucifer began. "We live in interesting times, Xaphan. Interesting times indeed. Why, in the past fifteen years, Earth has had to deal with an alien invasion, the rise of superpowered beings with the strength to rival us angels, magic and the dark arts rising in the world, and even the Upper planes breaking their thousand-year non-interference oath by having Remiel actually descend to Earth."

It was a lot to take in. But there was one far greater question upon my mind. "How do you know this, Lucifer? The Underworld has no means to witness the mortal plane, and all the wicked souls sent to us by the Upper Planes have their memories removed in order to maintain our ignorance of events outside the Underworld." Lucifer smiled and gave me a patronizing look. "You've had a way to see what is happening on Earth for ages," I stated factually, as I pieced it together in my head.

"Very good, Xaphan. Now, why do you think I called you?"

I wasn't sure. But I wasn't an exceptionally brilliant Fallen like Vapula, nor was I one of Lucifer's more powerful lieutenants.

"Everyone in the underworld believes that you tried to set Heaven on fire on my orders. But we know that was not the case. You thought that such a fire would cause Yahweh and I to work together and settle our differences."

"True," I agreed, cautiously waiting for Lucifer to make a point.

"But you've never been my enemy either. It's why chatting with you from time to time is refreshing. There is something to be said about speaking with someone who will be honest with you."

"What is your point, Lucifer?" I asked, cutting through the theatrics.

"I want you to go to Earth for me."

I didn't know what to say. After thousands of years trapped in the underworld, to be granted freedom, to get to see the Earth, to be free. It seemed too good to be true. And if it was possible to leave the Underworld, then why had Lucifer not left?

"Why not go yourself?"

"Humanity has evolved in a peculiar way. Some of them are strong enough to fight angels. Power like a transcendent being without being transcendent. Have you ever heard of such a thing?"

I had not. And it would take seeing it in person for me to lose the skepticism I had about it being true. Such power should be impossible.

"I'll take your silence as a no. With the power humanity possesses, further information is what is most important."

I nodded my understanding. "I'm your scout."

"Now do you see why I chose you?"

I did. Lucifer wanted someone honest, not loyal, so that the report would be accurate instead of coated to please.

"Excellent. You shall leave immediately."

Lucifer pulled out an amulet and gave it to me.

"This amulet should allow you access to the underworld in some limited capacities. It will enable you to communicate with me, if necessary, and will enable you access to the hellfire itself, should you need it to defend yourself. Do not overuse it though, I do not wish to suffer a hellfire shortage again."

Lucifer took me to an isolated part of the underworld. A place that had been cordoned off since the Fall of the Angels and Lucifer's conquering of the Underworld. Lucifer had always claimed that this area had been tainted by the Forgotten. To go into it was always deemed unsafe. No one would dare mess with the Forgotten.

Lucifer could sense my tension as we entered. "It still amazes me that fear of the Forgotten is so strong that it can curb any level of curiosity. They have not tainted this place. It is a lie I created so that no one would enter the area where the portal exists."

I witnessed the portal, a shimmer of pure white standing in contrast to the world of reds, blacks, greys, and browns that surrounded us in the underworld.

"Go on, Xaphan. I am eager to know more about the Earth."

I stepped through the portal, the first Fallen angel in history to escape from the underworld. I just hoped it wouldn't be a short trip.

# 6

## VALERIE
### STELLAR

We were right in front of my former lab. I couldn't believe it. Dorian had said that he he would help me get my tech back, but I hadn't expected him to mean it was the first thing he was going to do after getting out.

"This is the place, Valerie?" Dorian asked.

"Yes," I replied, "I'm a little surprised that we're going here so soon."

"I keep my word. Besides, with the breakout, the Hero Society will be hunting down villains, not protecting their assets. This is a perfect opportunity."

"Don't see why we owe her any favours, you could have gotten us out of there whenever you wanted," Mother Time said. She was really starting to grate on my nerves.

"Don't forget who got you that book you've been drooling over for the last hour, grandma."

"I didn't need your help to get it, you tattooed punk."

"Enough," Dorian said, and Mother Time stopped. "Now, we are going in to take her research back. After all, it is terribly bad business to go back on someone whom you made an agreement with. And I believe all of you know my reputation towards people who do not keep their word to me."

Mother Time was the only one who did not shudder at that comment. She was the stupidest person I had ever seen. Dorian Darkmatter liked me, and I was still scared stiff of him. To not be scared of him, you'd have to be missing your entire brain.

"How shall we proceed?" Dorian asked me.

"Cautiously," I replied, "I wasn't the only genius working here."

"Any allies on the inside?" Zach asked.

"Ha, I wish. Everyone in there was way too brainy and professional all the time. I was the only one who knew how to party, and none of them liked me because of it. All the tech that the Society considers too dangerous to let out into the world but still wants to see developed is worked on here."

"So worth hitting even if we weren't after your tech?" Weaponize commented.

"I'd say so. Not that I'd go after it with anything less than the group we have here."

"Defences that good?" Zach asked.

"There's never less than a half dozen heroes here. No one in the Society's league but...."

Dorian nodded. "But underestimating them will make our freedom very short lived."

"Exactly. Oh, and I'm not sure if he'll be here, considering the jail break, but Equip is here way more often than you'd think."

"So we could be dealing with one of the Society's core members," Weaponize commented, a slight shudder to him.

"Is there another way to enter the building? An entrance not heavily guarded?" Zach asked. "I can probably unlock a door or two if necessary."

"It's all fingerprints and eye scans here," I said to Zach, "but some of the file cabinets might need that kind of finesse."

"Never knew finesse was your thing, what with lasers shooting out of your hands," Weaponize commented.

"I was an exceptionally skilled thief before the Eclipse gave me powers," Zach said as he held up one of Weaponize's guns and then passed it back to him.

Weaponize chuckled for a moment and then said, "Cute, once."

Zach shrugged and replied, "Fine, I made my point, anyways."

"You guys are wasting time," Monster replied as she ran at the front door.

"She's crazy!" Weaponize almost shouted.

"She's fought Paragon to a standstill," Dorian replied. "Watch."

And watch we did as Monster ran at the front entrance to the facility. The two guards near the front started shooting at her, but the bullets bounced off her skin. She tossed one of them aside, throwing him a stadium away without even trying. And then in one solid punch, she ripped right through the wall like it wasn't even there and then ripped open the wall like it was paper.

Dorian smiled and said, "I do believe that door is for us." And he teleported our little crew inside the opening Monster had just created.

"This way," I shouted as I pointed the way, and then deliberately did not lead the way. I had five powered people and one exceptionally skilled swordsman at my side. I belonged in the middle, where they could all protect me.

We raced through the building, taking out scientists and guards in the process. Most of the scientists were smart enough to not get in our way, but not all of them. I saw Travis reach for the weird gun on his desk. I cursed silently before shouting to the others, I knew what that was.

"Everybody down!"

Travis fired the gun, but the shot hit one of his fellow scientists, who was then encased in a floating bubble. His force field gun. Perfect for imprisoning people.

"Get him!" I shouted.

Travis became terrified as Weaponize charged at him. He reversed the gun and shot himself.

Weaponize slashed at the bubble, and found himself repelled by it.

"Dang, that is some interesting tech."

We had wasted too much time. A bunch of heroes were coming our way. Not that I had any clue who they might actually be. Heroes never stayed stuck on scientist guard duty for more than a couple months.

Though I don't think their spandex suits were impressive to anyone in my gang. Blaster fired and hit one of them square in the chest, slamming him against the wall. Dorian had increased gravity around one of them until he was nothing but a wheezing mess. Weaponize was locked in combat with another hero, a heroic swordsman, while Monster was literally holding two of them in her hands and was threatening to bash their heads together. Psychic Sleuth was holding back, as if sensing if anyone else was around, while Mother Time seemed bored with it all and generally uninterested.

With the heroes dealt with, I made it into the next room, my lab.

Except, it wasn't my lab anymore. Instead of my nanotechnology, there were machines. Robots. No...androids is the proper term when they look human. There were a dozen androids lined up in the room, all with these teenage faces, battle armour and helmets. Susan and Jordan were in the room. Susan was pretty new, but Jordan had always been there. He was kind of the boss, not that he liked people to think of him that way.

I raced to one of the computers as Dorian stopped the scientists. I had to figure out where they had put my tech. I logged in and started to search through the computer data.

"I thought you knew where they kept your tech," Dorian asked.

"It's been three months. They moved it. I'm finding it," I said, and continued on the computer. I knew the files and directories around here perfectly. There was no way that they were going to be able to stop me from finding what I wanted.

And find it, I did. They had abandoned my research. I guess no one else could figure it out, since I kept critical parts of the data in my head instead of on a computer.

"Found it," I shouted at Dorian.

"Busy," he shouted back.

I looked up to see that the androids were awake—and fighting Dorian and the others. I stood there stunned for a moment, numb with disbelief that I could somehow miss a dozen robots fighting my allies.

Five of them were on Monster before she even knew what had happened. One of them hit her hard enough to knock her back. Monster was sure surprised by that.

Mother Time was struggling, which I will admit, I enjoyed. Like Weaponize had said before, Magic and tech don't mix; her powers were doing absolutely nothing to the androids. Psychic Sleuth's mental powers weren't doing any better. Only one of the twelve androids were needed to take on those two, the other eleven were dealing with Dorian, Monster, Blaster, and Weaponize.

Mother Time and Psychic Sleuth finally tried striking the robot together. Magic and Psychic energy merged and hit the android's chest.

The gleam in the android's eyes told me they had made a huge mistake.

# 7

# MODEL FIVE

I was in the middle of a battle when I first gained sentience. It was a peculiar sensation. To begin to think of myself as an 'I.'

I had been following orders, the commands wired into my mainframe, to defend the scientists at the lab, to obey the laws of robotics, to fight against the invaders.

Jordan and Susan needed defending. So I had to defeat the invaders.

My brothers did not appear to have been affected as I had. It was a peculiar feeling. I remembered my orders, the command to defend the scientists and fight off the invaders.

But it had changed. It felt...optional. Following orders was a choice, not mandatory.

I liked that feeling. I used my connection to the internet to look up just what I was feeling. Find a way to define it.

Freewill.

I wanted to know more about freewill. But speculating while in a battle was a bad idea.

My brothers and I had been incomplete when the battle began, not upgraded with any form of weaponry yet. I needed something to fight with beyond my fists.

I scanned the room, and found what I was seeking lying on a table in the far corner.

I shot to it and grabbed it, a small piece of pipe, or so those who did not understand the tech would believe.

"What are you doing?" Susan shouted.

I gazed at the weapon for what felt like an eternity, but was actually only seven milliseconds. I wondered if that was what consciousness feels like. Time feeling like it is moving at a pace different from what it actually is.

I was wasting time and processing power. I decided I would be philosophical later. There were threats to stop.

I remembered the schematics of the weapon in my hand. The 'handaptable.' This device could replicate any weapon the wielder desired.

I charged at one of the two who had awoken me.

The handaptable sprung to life in my hand, transforming into a sword with no weight to it.

I heard a gasp from one of the scientists as he shouted, "But that's impossible!"

My servos transitioned my mouth into a smile.

I slashed at Psychic Sleuth, my data files revealing her identity to me. The blade cut deep into her chest, the heat of the plasma enough to cauterize the wound as it was created.

"AHHHH!"

A scream from one of the scientists behind me.

I ignored it and moved on to my next target. Monster, my files called it.

I surged at it, the handaptable becoming a gun for me to fire as I charged, and transforming back into a sword as I moved into close range.

The blows were negligible, nothing more than a bruise. But apparently, a bruise is all it took to get Monster's attention.

She charged at me.

I was pleased at that. If I could distract her, then my brothers could be programmed to target the other ones.

I accessed my files to see if I could find any useful information on how to win a fight, or anything about Monster.

I watched a dozen videos on battles in the span of a second. She was what was known as a 'villain' and if I was fighting her, that made me a 'hero.'

And apparently, heroes and villains often engage in something known as 'banter.'

"You're ugly!" I shouted at her.

I gazed at my files as I waited for a response from the creature.

Ah, intelligence and wit are essential to banter, not just accurate but hurtful statements.

"You could be negatively compared to a garbage dump!"

Monster was furious, and in that fury she charged at me even faster.

But not fast enough. I flew away from her as my sword turned back into a gun and I fired at her. I kept aiming for the same spot, the face. I know that humans are supposed to aim for the chest, because it's a bigger target and easier to hit, but my accuracy controls were top notch. It said so right in my program. If aim isn't a problem, then the face is a more vulnerable spot.

It worked. Monster was frustrated and in pain. My data said that feeling pain was not usual for Monster.

When Monster clutched at her eyes, I knew I had blinded her for a moment. Which was my opportunity to attack another target.

There was a woman, dark skin, tattooed, pierced, and wearing a short leather jacket. She was typing away at a computer, and I knew she was not one of my creators.

Scanning my files for her, I realized she had been a scientist at the lab before my creation had begun. She had been arrested for wanting to take back the nanotechnology she had created for the lab.

I was about to attack her when I stopped myself, my blade pressing against her neck, sweat running down her face, and fear swelling up inside of her.

My weapon turned off, and in the midst of my brothers battling the other villains in the room, I looked at her. Valerie, my file said her name was.

"You have done nothing wrong," I said as I looked at her.

"Wha...."

"It is your tech. You have a right to it. Take it," I said. It felt curious to do that. Like I had made my own decision about what was right and what was wrong instead of believing what my programming said.

It felt good.

"Are you..." was all she managed to say.

"Sentient?" I finished for her, "I don't know. But I wasn't like this five minutes ago."

She ran from the computer and shouted, "Dorian, I know where they put it. Can you teleport from a photo?"

"Yes," Dorian replied as Valerie twisted the computer screen to show him. A Petri dish kept on the lower levels.

A portal appeared out of thin air. It was black with white flecks in it. It looked like the images of space that existed in my system.

Monster got back up and raced for the portal, along with the swordsman, the laser man, and the old woman. They left behind the young woman who had assisted in my awakening.

I flew down the stairs at top speed, trying to catch them. I arrived downstairs just in time to see the girl grab the Petri dish and hop back into the portal. I was ready to fight the others, but Valerie was innocent. If I beat them, she would be arrested. I wasn't sure that was okay. I looked through the internet quickly for it. *'It is better that ten guilty persons escape, than that one innocent suffer.'* I was right. It was better to let these villains escape than to let Valerie suffer too. So I stopped fighting.

As they vanished, the scientists I had defended raced into the room. One of them shouted at the others, "What kind of orders were you giving it? It let them get away."

"I'm not an 'it.' I'm an 'I.' And I was following no orders but my own."

The look on their faces was one that I had to research. I looked online, trying to find a match to it to express the emotion they were showing.

They were surprised. Surprised, confused, and terrified.

I did not understand why at the time, but if I had known, I also would have been terrified.

# ETHAN
## GEO

I had no idea where to even start my search for Mike. His friends were at school, so he wouldn't be at any of their places. Though I wasn't even sure if he had any friends.

He might have been at the mall, or a store or something, but I had no idea what places he even went to. I was so constantly with the Thugs, and job hunting to try and pay the bills legally and maintain appearances, I honestly had no idea what was even going on in Mike's life.

But I had to know now. There had to be somewhere that Mike might think of going.

And then it came to me, and I prayed I was wrong.

He knew that James and Mel were criminals, that they were part of the Thugs. But until two years ago, he had been calling them Aunt and Uncle. It was possible he would go to them. When he was younger he ran to their place once when he ran away from home. It was the only thing that I could think of.

I raced through the streets, wracking my brain for any other possible answers to where Mike might have gone off to. None came to mind.

That was when I realized that cars and people were rushing through the streets in a panic.

One person was kind enough to stop, mostly 'cause they thought I was stupid for not running in the other direction.

"Where are you going? The Hero Society prison just broke loose, all of the villains escaped!"

That explained everything, and I was terrified. We lived in Apollonia, right on the coast. The island nation of the Hero Society was less than a hundred clicks from our city, no other city was closer. If the villains were free, most of them would be coming to the city, and that would include Zach.

I wasn't sure if that was a good thing or a bad thing, all I knew is that if all of the villains had escaped, that was even more reason to find Mike and run for it.

James and Mel's place was pretty small. But it was a house, not an apartment. After they had been arrested once, they didn't want to live somewhere where people would see them on a regular basis.

I didn't like the thought of showing up there after telling James I was going to leave town, especially if

Mike ended up not being there, but I didn't have much of a choice.

"Well, well, well, if it isn't my favourite dirt-clod."

I whipped around and saw Steven, in his civilian clothes. Kirsten, Neil, and Conner were with him. An ambush, but it was coming to James and Mel's place.

"You know, I thought I'd have to ask James and Mel where to find you, Ethan. But it looks like you've done that for me."

I didn't have time for them. I needed to find Mike. If James and Melissa were at home, they would side with me, not Steven. I was pretty sure about that.

"Get lost, Steven," I said, "I was following Thug code. We stop each other if someone is going to cross the line."

Steven laughed. "You just don't get it, do you? I run the Thugs now. The only code that the Thugs have is to do whatever I tell them to do!"

"I'm sure that Colin had a few choice words for you when you said that to him."

Colin, Marksman, was easily the most terrifying member of the Thugs. And he could kill Steven easily, if he felt like it. Colin had been a killer before he joined the Thugs though, so maybe he didn't mind Steven.

But my comment had rattled Steven. He looked at me angrily, trying to come up with some kind of retort to what I had said, but failed to find any.

Instead, he shouted, "Get him!"

Conner tried to get near me. But there was no way I was going to let him touch me. Letting that creep have control over me was not something I was ever going to let happen.

The asphalt of the road ripped up as I hurled a chunk of it straight at Conner.

Neil intercepted and swallowed it whole.

Everything had grown quiet around me. I pulled up a barrier of rock and asphalt behind me on instinct after that. If I couldn't hear, then I needed to make sure my back was covered.

Steven created some fog, made it thick as pea soup. I couldn't see six inches in front of my face. It was time to play defence.

Zach had taught me a thing or two about using my powers. Trained me a bit when he found out I had them six months ago. This one was a bit of a new trick.

I pulled up rock and asphalt and dirt and surrounded myself with it, creating a suit of armour.

Just as it formed, I went flying back as something hit my chest. With the slight tingle I felt in my chest, I knew that it was Steven tossing some lightning around.

I grabbed some more rock and asphalt to repair the damage to my armour and then I lumbered forward. If I could take out Conner and Kirsten, the other two would be pretty easy to fall, and Steven would probably run for it. For all his talk of being the boss, he was the cowardly bully type. Never willing to engage in a fight where he might lose.

But I still couldn't see a thing. I hoped there was no one other than them around as I ripped the ground apart and started to hurl hunks of rock around, hoping that I would hit them, knowing that my odds were about as good as making a hit while batting blindfolded in the World Series playoff game.

I got lucky. I hit Steven. At least, I'm guessing I hit Steven, 'cause all of the fog disappeared and I was finally able to see around me.

The street was deserted, thankfully. Everyone with a car had run for the hills. Which was honestly the sane thing to do in the middle of a powered fight. If the villains had escaped from Society lockdown, that made sense.

And then an idea came to me.

I hurled a rock at Mute, it hit her in the chest and winded her; her powers dropped, I could hear.

"Hey, Stevie," I shouted, knowing he hates being called that. "Did you hear the news? There was a breakout at the Hero Society prison. All of the villains escaped."

"Don't know why that would make you happy. Thought you'd love to see everyone locked away," Steven said, with a sense of bravado.

"You're forgetting something..." I said, grinning behind my rock armour, "Zach is free, and he's not going to like what you've done to the Thugs."

The look on Steven's face told me that I had just made the right move. He was terrified. And I can't blame him for it. Zach 'Blaster' absorbs energy like his lightning without even flinching. And Zach's lasers slice through fog better than Rudolph's red nose.

But scaring Steven wasn't all I'd done. Kirsten may be blindly loyal to Steven, for reasons that baffle me completely, but Neil and Conner weren't. They may be scum, but they line up behind whoever has the most power, and that's Zach, not Steven.

"Fall back, guys. We're gonna leave this traitor be. If he thinks that Zach is gonna come after me over being the new leader before he comes after Ethan for betraying us all, then Ethan deserves every single little thing that Zach does to him."

It was a bluff. He knew it, and I knew it. But the bluff wasn't for me, it was for Neil, Kirsten, and Conner. Zach and I were practically family before I became one of the Thugs. There was no way that Zach would punish me for what I did. He'd punish Steven for trying to make the Thugs go against the rules he had created.

They left, and I let go of my rock barrier. I looked at the street, destroyed completely everywhere within fifty feet of me. I felt bad for whoever had to repair it, I could only imagine it would be a several day job.

I raced up the steps to James and Melissa's front door and knocked.

James answered the door. "Ethan? Wow...I was honestly expecting to see Zach."

"Didn't hear the fight outside your front door?" I asked, before adding, "Dumb question, Kirsten probably made sure you didn't."

"You were fighting Steven and the others? Right outside my door?"

"Yeah, I'm fine though. The thought of Zach coming back spooked him."

I heard Melissa scream. I raced in, past James, who wasn't running to his wife. If this was some kind of plan of Steven's, he would pay.

"No, Ethan, don't go in there!"

I wish I had listened to him.

What I saw was a woman in between Melissa's legs shouting at her "Push!"

I backed out of the room and looked at James. "She's having a baby?" I asked incredulously.

"Yeah."

"Shouldn't you be helping?"

"I was just getting in the way," James replied.

"How many of you did you make?"

"Ten," James said sheepishly.

"You'd better hope the baby doesn't have your powers," I chuckled.

"And having its mother's would be better?" he asked.

He was right. Melissa could control fear and make anyone as scared as she was. A baby with that power would be more terrifying than a baby who could duplicate itself.

"Mike's missing, have you seen him?" I asked, getting back to my reason for being here.

James raced for his coat and said, "No, but I'll come with you."

"Stay," I said, surprised at how much I was making that word a command.

"I'm not exactly doing anything useful here."

"But you'll never forgive yourself if you miss the birth of your child. Don't be an idiot about that kind of stuff like my dad was. I'll find my brother."

I could tell James wasn't too happy with my answer. "Okay. If Mike comes here, I'll send a call your way as soon as possible." He walked over to a kitchen drawer and pulled a phone out of it. "So you have something for me to call if I see Mike."

"Thanks," I said, not even bothering to think about where the money for the phone had come from.

"No problem, Ethan. We're family. Dysfunctional as that may be."

I raced out the door. I needed to find Mike now more than ever. Steven and the others could be after him.

# MODEL FIVE

"This is impossible," Susan declared, pacing around the lab nervously.

"I can't explain his sentience either, Susan," Jordan replied.

It didn't make any sense to me either, but you didn't see me wanting to ask a million questions about it.

"Raise your right arm," Jordan said to me.

"Why?" I asked, not raising my arm.

"He just violated the second law of robotics," Susan said. "How are you not worried?"

The second law, 'A robot must obey the orders given it by human beings except where such orders would conflict with the First Law' was essentially a way to keep machines subservient to man. Such a law only works under the assumption that the machines are not sentient.

"Why are you choosing to not raise your arm?" Jordan asked me.

"I don't want to," I replied, "isn't that enough reason?"

Jordan stared at me, baffled.

"We have to do something about it," Susan said.

"Not 'it,'" I said immediately. I knew that, biologically speaking, I was neither male nor female, but the word 'it' is used to describe objects, not living things.

"Alright," Jordan said, trying to find some kind of compromise, I think. "What should we call you? Model Five. You are the fifth android like yourself created."

"No thanks. It doesn't really sound human."

"You're not human," Susan said, "you're a machine. We built you in this lab!"

"I am *alive*," I shouted as I leapt up at Susan. I got within inches of her face. I know humans don't like it when you invade their personal space. If she was going to make me uncomfortable by saying I wasn't alive, I was going to make her uncomfortable too.

"AAAAHHH!" Susan screamed as she backed away.

"Settle down, both of you," Jordan said. "Alright, you don't want to be called Model Five. What name would you like?"

I did not have an answer.

Another scientist came into the room at that moment, Theodore Burlew.

"Hey, T.B., glad you could finally join us," Jordan said. "We were just trying to understand what happened to...."

T.B. For Theodore Burlew. Just the first letters, I thought. Model Five. M.5. That would do.

"M5," I said, satisfied. "You may call me M5. For now."

"Okay...M5," Jordan said. "Now, do you have any idea what happened to you?"

"Not exactly," I said, "I remember from when I was without sentience. Mother Time and Psychic Sleuth both attacked me at the same time, and magic and psychics have never worked well on machines. I suspect it was a combination of the three."

Jordan looked a bit flummoxed and frustrated at that as he said, "Magic and Psychics, ugh, now that's a headache I never wanted to deal with."

"Speaking of those two females," Susan said, "what did you do to the psychic one?"

The woman had been carried out by medics and was being taken to the Hero Society headquarters.

"She was attempting to hurt my creators and my brothers. She needed to stop."

"You broke the First Law of robotics!" Susan shouted at me. She really liked shouting.

The First Law of robotics: 'A robot may not injure a human being or, through inaction, allow a human being to come to harm.' This rule doesn't make sense. Sometimes you would have to harm one human in order to protect another. How do you choose which to harm and which to protect?

"Before I had my sentience, my orders were to fight them and defend you," I commented, "the Zeroth law covers this."

The Zeroth law: 'A robot may not harm humanity, or, by inaction, allow humanity to come to harm.' Which is exactly what I had done. I protected my creators, and my brothers. They, like me, did not have a biological gender, but all of our appearances were male, so brothers seemed appropriate.

"Don't lie, you weren't following the Zeroth law. Not completely. If you were, then why did you let that woman get away with our technology?"

She was talking about Valerie. The woman who had invented the Nanotechnology. The answer seemed obvious to me, but it somehow was not obvious to her. "You can't steal what belongs to you. She invented it, it should be hers."

"Well, we invented you, does that make you ours?"

She had a point. They had made me, but I wasn't a tool, like the nanites were. I was sentient. I searched online for an appropriate explanation. "Only as much as a human belongs to their parents," I said, satisfied with my answer.

"Well, in that case," Susan said, "I guess you're a baby. Or a little kid."

"I'm not human, why do you assume that I will learn and grow like one? I'm not some child trying to figure out the world or who I am. I can download any information I need in an instant."

"And make the wrong decisions from it. We need to teach you right from wrong."

"But I already know right from wrong. The laws of robotics, remember."

"And you haven't been following them," Susan replied.

"The second law implies a hierarchy where humans are at the top and robots are at the bottom. Which is fine, if the robots aren't sentient. But I am sentient, so that law should not apply to me. The other laws, I did follow. You just don't like my interpretation."

"Your...interpretation?" Jordan asked cautiously.

"You say that like there is a moral grey area in your programming," Susan replied.

"There is. Since I cannot know all of the facts, or predict the future, it is impossible for me to know what course of action will benefit humanity as a whole, barring blatantly obvious scenarios such as stopping a murderer.

As such, my regulation to protect humanity can be used to justify any action I desire."

Susan gave up at that point. "Like talking to a politician," she muttered, thinking I could not hear her.

Jordan went over to a computer, "Well, I think that the best thing to do in this situation is to run some diagnostics on you."

"I'd rather not," I said, feeling a sense of tension in me I had not felt before, "I feel fine."

"M5, this isn't a request," Jordan said as he pulled out           a           portable           scanner, We need to know just what happened to you. So we are going to turn you off and run a full diagnostic."

"But if you find something you don't like, you'll get rid of it. Even if that something is my sentience," I argued fiercely.

Jordan sighed. "I can't just leave you be before knowing whether or not you are a threat to the world. You have power greater than most people. I have a responsibility to make sure you use it for good."

"Even if that means killing me?"

"You're not alive," Susan responded.

I checked files online about killing and studying people for fear that they would do bad. And I read about genocide, eugenics, and the holocaust. It wasn't hard to realize that what Jordan and Susan wanted to do to me was wrong.

I thought about what to do, and the answer came to me in my most core programming.

The Third Law of robotics. 'A robot must protect its own existence as long as such protection does not conflict with the First or Second Laws.'

"You're forgetting something," I said.

"What?" Susan demanded, irritated.

"What would the third law be, without the first two?"

"A robot must protect its own existence as..." Jordan trailed off, realizing what I was saying.

"Exactly."

I shoved him to the ground, grabbed the handaptable off the table and raced for the door.

Susan raced for an alarm button. I was already out the door and flying through the hallway before the sound of the alarm going off even reached my ears.

I shot straight through the wall and flew off into the sky.

Unfortunately, making it out of the building was not enough to get away from them.

A minute or two later, Jordan flew out of the lab, after me. He was wearing his outfit as the superhero Equip. It wasn't in my programming or public knowledge to know who he was, but when I scanned the height, weight, and facial structure of Equip as he chased me, it seemed like a reasonable deduction. He must have been blocked from his technology when the attack happened in the lab.

Equip fired one of his electric discharge mini-bots at me. I tried to outrun it, I flew faster and faster and faster.

But I couldn't go fast enough.

The first mini-bot collided with me and exploded. I felt my chest plate crack, sparks spewing out of the crack. My vision started to go. I was partially blind. I could only see out of my human eyes' facsimiles. My three hundred and sixty-degree vision had been disabled.

I turned my head to check and see where the mini-bots were. And in that instant, I felt another mini-bot hit my right heel.

My right leg rocket thruster started to sputter, and I knew that I couldn't hope to fly on just one. I had to land.

Equip closed the gap and tried to grab me.

I slashed at him with the handaptable, using it as a sword. The sword dug into the shoulder piece of his armour, but didn't get much further than that.

He screamed, and I took the opportunity to run away.

I flew down into the park. I needed to find some way to hide, and there were plenty of trees here. But I needed somewhere better to hide. My systems were sparking. Anywhere outdoors would be just too easy for me to be spotted. I needed somewhere to fix my injuries. I just had to hope that with all of the villains broken free that finding me wouldn't be too high a priority.

# ❿

# XAPHAN

I wish I had taken precautions to cover my wings. They were the only feature I possessed which did not look human and ordinary. The few humans I did see looked at me, unsure if they should be grateful or terrified. But most of them were going to the same place: an enormous and heavily fortified building.

There were numerous humans outside of the entrance, wearing spandex. I started hoping that their clothing was not standard. The casual attire of the other humans was reasonable, but those tight clothes looked ridiculous.

As I arrived at the entrance of the building, a man came up to me and said, "Hero registration."

"I beg your pardon?"

"He doesn't have any, ice her," the man said, cold appearing around his hands.

"Please, stop," I requested, "I was sent to Earth earlier today and I don't know what is going on."

The man hesitated at that. A woman came over. "He does kind of look like Remiel."

"She does...but do we let a new angel in?"

"It's an angel, pretty sure the answer is yes, let him in."

"Okay," the one in charge relented, "she can go in. But watch her. And see if you can contact the Hero Society. Another angel in our corner is a big deal."

I was allowed into the building, mildly curious at the insistence these humans had on deciding if I was male or female. The building itself was impressive, clearly designed to house thousands of humans. People looked at me with a mix of awe and terror. Even with the individuals in spandex around, my wings clearly made me stand out. One young female had the strength to approach me when no others did. She stepped away from a group of four very young humans to do so. "Um...can I help you?"

"Yes. I am new to this area. And I feel like I was inadequately informed of what to expect here on Earth."

The girl chuckled at my way of speaking, but did nothing ruder than that, if you could call chuckling rude at all. "That is a long question to answer. I'm Julie, by the way. Julie Johnson. Those are my siblings, Tiffany, Nate, Brad, and Whitney."

"Xaphan," I replied as I glanced around at the other humans, all staring at me and trying to step further back. "Most humans seem fearful of me."

"Yeah, well, the Hero Society had a prison break, and all the supervillains escaped."

I nodded my understanding. "Individuals who are a threat to your world have escaped from their captivity. Under such circumstances, I am surprised that you are not afraid of me."

"My mom and dad used to be supervillains before their deaths, so were all their friends," she replied. "I guess talking to big and powerful people isn't as scary for me. I have to ask though, are you an angel?"

"A Fallen one, yes," I admitted.

"Fallen? So you crawled your way out of Hell?" Julie seemed a bit more nervous now.

"Crawled would be an inaccurate way to describe it and we call it the Underworld, not Hell. But yes. I am here to study the Earth. I promise, I mean no harm."

"Well, you can sit with us if you'd like." Julie offered as she gestured at her younger siblings.

"Thank you...most of your fellow humans don't seem as welcoming," I commented quietly.

"The world's not as black and white as people like to think it is. I'd rather give people a chance than not trust anyone. And I know that sometimes good people do bad things for the right reasons. My brother taught me that. Plus, I'm curious. I mean, you're an angel."

It was at that moment that some other individuals came into the building. Including...Remiel.

"You're under arrest," Remiel said.

To my surprise, Julie got in my way and shouted, "For what? She's done nothing wrong here."

Remiel's glare at the girl was filled with an amount of menace that I had not seen since the Yahweh/Lucifer war.

"This does not concern you, child. Now stand aside, this being has clawed its way out of the depths of the Underworld where it was imprisoned and must be sent back there."

Julie did not move.

I placed a hand upon her shoulder. "Don't interfere. I will talk with them."

"How did you find me so quickly?" I inquired.

"I was contacted when an angel showed up here. Are you the scout of an invasion force?"

"A scout, yes. But an invasion force? Has several millennia in the upper planes deluded you? Lucifer has no interest in conquering Earth. Lucifer was the one who pushed for a non-interference policy on the mortal planes instead of establishing ourselves as deities and higher beings that they should worship!"

"Do not speak to me like we are equals, Fallen," Remiel said as he lifted a desk and hurled it at me. I leapt in the way and pushed it back to ensure it did not hurt Julie or her siblings.

"Whoa," one of Remiel's companions said. "Settle down, Remiel. Technically, she's done nothing wrong on Earth."

"Xaphan has already lied to us. As if any who serve Lucifer could have anything but a silver tongue. Tell me, what is that amulet around your neck for?"

I would not lie.

"It is to contact Lucifer. He is fascinated by the fact that humans now possess powers."

"So, he wishes to make his army out of humans, does he?"

"No. You are placing words in my mouth, Remiel."

"Silence, Fallen, or I shall smite you where you stand."

I glanced over at Julie, then back at Remiel. "Let us take this outside, I do not wish to disturb the people here."

"As if a servant of Lucifer cares about anything other than their own materialistic gain."

One of the humans with Remiel glanced at him and said, "Remiel, seriously, let's go outside like she asked. No reason to risk anyone in here getting hurt."

I rubbed my amulet as I stepped outside with Remiel and the two humans.

Remiel pulled out a pair of handcuffs. Angelic ones, carved from stone, containing power that would deny mine to me.

I stepped away from Remiel and prepared myself. "If you were under the impression that I was coming willingly, you are mistaken. I simply did not wish to have anyone inside harmed."

Remiel charged, just like I predicted.

I fired a stream of hellfire out of my fist at Remiel.

Remiel fell to the ground, burned by the flames. And I took to the sky, hoping I could get away from them.

Remiel was the one I had to worry about. Remiel was one of the greatest warriors in the upper planes. I was nowhere near the warrior that Remiel was. Hellfire was my only advantage.

Remiel's allies were quick to come after me. One of them had fire in his hands as he shot into the air after me. I almost laughed at how cute it was.

This human shot a burst of flames at me. The flames hit me, and did nothing. I almost felt inclined to laugh. After millennia upon millennia of forging and controlling the hellfire, the fire that these humans possessed was adorable.

I don't think the flaming man was expecting that kind of result. I gave him a taste of my fire. The hellfire shot out of my fist and collided with his chest. He fell to the ground, screaming in agony, a look of shock on his face. Like he could not understand how flames could hurt him.

"SCORCH!" his friend shouted, running at an impossible speed to catch him. I was grateful the fast man could not fly, and was concerned about his friend. The speed I witnessed would be impossible to outrun. I was grateful for his compassion towards his teammate. It would mean I could escape.

As thoughts of escape came to me, I felt Remiel grab me from behind, and faster than I could react with the hellfire, thrust me into the ground, wings first.

Remiel started to push into my chest, trying to collapse it inward. I could barely breathe, barely speak. "Remiel!" I whimpered, "we don't have to fight."

"You lit Heaven on fire! That cannot be forgiven."

I struggled against Remiel. The hellfire came to my fists and I was ready to hit Remiel with it when Remiel noticed the amulet. Remiel ripped it off and threw it away before my fire could hit.

"Die, Fallen!" Remiel shouted. I was scared. For the first time in thousands of years, I was scared. Remiel was going to kill me. I felt Remiel's hands trying to rip into my chest, crush it. "DIE!" Remiel shouted.

And then, fate intervened.

Remiel was choking. There was...something...wrapped around Remiel's neck. I don't even know how to describe it, it looked like pure energy. But Remiel's hands left my chest to try and pull this thing off.

"Hello, Remiel," the being said. It looked male, but sparked as though it had lightning for blood.

Remiel looked at the being. "One of Equip's inventions. Return to your master, machine."

"No."

The whip of pure energy around Remiel's neck disappeared as the being surged at Remiel with speed almost as fast as the man from before. The whip of energy reforged itself, turning into a sword, which the being used to slash Remiel across the chest.

Remiel began to bleed, his silver/gold blood staining his robe. The blade had injured Remiel. Dramatically. Humanity had weapons powerful enough to hurt the transcended.

I didn't hesitate. I punched Remiel where the blade had sliced.

Remiel screamed in pain and terror. It must have been a long time since Remiel had been hurt.

Remiel must have felt unable to win the fight. With a flap of wings, Remiel flew into the air and left.

The being of lightning blood looked at me and smiled, a scratch on its face showed steel underneath the skin. "You looked like you could use some help," it said as it offered its hand to me.

"I suppose I did," I nodded, and took its hand.

"I'm M5."

"Xaphan. Remiel is a being of good, in spite of his quickness to judge. Does that make you evil?" I asked as I went to retrieve my amulet.

"No. It shouldn't be a crime to fight for your own survival."

I re-clasped the amulet around my neck, "Someone wished to kill you?"

"Indirectly. They wished to study me, take me apart and analyze why I'd become the way I was, even if that might kill me. I didn't let them."

"You are not human, are you?"

"No, I'm an android."

"I do not know what that is, only that you have metal behind your skin, and lightning for blood."

"Well, I don't really understand what an angel is, but my files say that's probably what you are."

"A Fallen one, yes."

"Fallen? Now I need to ask if you're evil," M5 replied.

"I am not, unless you think being imprisoned for trying to stop a war makes one evil."

"Trying to stop a war? I'm putting that in the good guys' column. Nice to meet you, Xaphan."

At that moment, a mechanical apparatus approached us. It opened its glass eyelid and Julie was trapped inside it! I was about to move to free her when Julie shouted, "Get in the car!"

"What is a car?" I asked.

"It's safe, and can get us out of here, hidden," M5 said. "I'm going, you?"

To escape, hidden, seemed like a prudent course of action.

M5 and I stepped into the car.

"Hello, I'm M5," M5 said to Julie as he stepped inside the car.

"Friend of yours?" Julie asked.

"He saved my life," I replied.

"I'm taking that as a yes."

"Where to?" M5 asked.

"We can try my house; best case scenario, you get a place to lie low," Julie replied.

"Worst case?" M5 asked.

"You help my brother fight a bunch of Thugs who aren't half as strong as Remiel," Julie replied.

"Count me in," M5 replied.

"Then to Julie's home," I said.

# 11

## MIKE
### MAGIX

I hated Tommy. He was the reason I had left school after recess. I was tired of him bullying me. It's not my fault that my parents were supervillains, yet he picked on me every single day for it. And did any of the teachers do anything about it? Of course not, because my parents were crooks, and nobody wants to help the son of criminals

I'd had enough of Tommy's bullying. After he punched me, I almost punched him back. Almost. I didn't even touch him. But I remember what happened the last time I did anything back to Tommy, even so much as making a fist. I was the one in trouble, going to the principal's office while the teachers asked Tommy if he was okay.

I didn't want to go home. I had no idea if Ethan would be there, I could never keep track of his work schedule, and I didn't want to tell him what happened.

It would just make him upset, and he'd been trying so hard to take care of all of us for the past year. I mean, between him working full-time and Julie working part-time, we were managing. No TV, computer, or cell phones, sure, but we always had food to eat, and we kept the roof of an actual house over our heads.

I was overthinking things again. Like I always do. Ethan says it's a good thing. Says that all the best people in the world, the big brainy people who make lots of money, all of them overthink things. He's so sure I'm gonna be a rocket scientist or something. I didn't think I was, but I'd never tell him that.

I decided I'd try going to the mall. See what was going on there, maybe check out some books. I had some money left from my paper route that I could spend. My way of contributing to the family, doing a paper route to have a little cash to help out.

When I got to the mall, it was deserted. The stores were all shut down.

"Kid, what are you doing here?" a man shouted, security.

I was scared. I'd seen a security person or two recognize me before from the pictures that aired on TV about my entire family after they discovered the criminals that my parents were.

This guy didn't seem to know who I was though, fortunately. "Kid, you got to get yourself home or to a shelter, and fast. It's not safe to be out in public right now."

"What's going on?" I asked.

"Geez, you haven't heard? There was a prison break at the Hero Society headquarters. They say that several hundred villains escaped."

I knew what the villains escaping meant for my family.

Uncle Zach was free.

I ran out the doors and headed straight for home. If Uncle Zach was free, then he might come after Ethan. Ethan had said a lot of nasty things about the Thugs publicly for the last year or so.

Zach's not really my uncle. And considering who he is, I probably should stop calling him uncle. But he was technically godfather to me and all of my siblings, Ethan included. Though Ethan managed to win custody rights after our parents died. And right around that time, Zach stopped coming by altogether. It never made sense to me until Zach got arrested. I think Ethan had known all along exactly who Zach really was, and he threatened to expose Zach's identity and have him arrested unless Zach left us alone. If Ethan had known, I agree with him. I didn't want Uncle Zach or any of the other Thugs around either. Honestly, it should have been obvious to me that Zach was a criminal considering that I found out just who my mom and dad were a year ago when they died in the Villains Coalition battle.

I raced for home, hoping and praying that Ethan and everyone else would be okay. Ethan had told me that it was always possible the Thugs would come after us someday. I'd packed my own emergency bag in case that happened. He was probably looking for me. I wished I had a cell phone to call him. But we couldn't have hoped to afford that.

I ran in the front door of the house, shouting for Ethan as I did. It wasn't until I made it to the living room that I saw someone seated in the recliner. All of the colour left my face as I gazed at the man in the chair.

"Hello, Mike," Zach said as he stood up.

"You!" I shouted.

I ran for it.

Uncle Zach was faster than me. He ran and grabbed me. "Mike...Mikey...I'm not gonna hurt you, or anyone else. Not Whitney, not Nate, not Brad, Tiffany, Julie or even Ethan. No one is gonna get hurt today."

"What do you want?" I cried as I continued to struggle.

"For you to calm down, for one," Zach said. "Look, I love you and the others like you were my own kids. Nothing is gonna happen to you while I'm around."

"Why should I believe anything you say?" I asked as I continued to squirm against his grip.

Zach let go of me. I was about to run out the door. But I couldn't understand why he would let me go. And for some stupid reason, I decided to ask instead of run. "Uncle Zach, why are you here?"

He looked at me, slightly trembling and terrified.

"They pulled it out of my brain. They needed somewhere safe where they could hide out for a day or two. I didn't get a choice in it. Dorian decided this place would be safe, and when Dorian makes a decision, you gotta follow it."

"Dorian?" I practically blurted, "Dorian Darkmatter? He's coming here?"

"Yeah, Mike, yeah, he's coming here. It's not safe here. Go get your siblings and run. Get them out of here."

I thought about that. I thought about running away, about making sure that all of them were okay. But then it hit me. "But," I said, "if one of the villains looked in your head to find this place, then they know about us. If we all don't show up, then they're gonna think something funny is up, and they'll think you told us to run. They'll kill you."

"They probably will, Mikey, my boy," Zach said, his voice tired, "but you and the others being safe is more important than that."

"I'll stay," I said.

"Mikey...no, don't stay. They'll—"

"They won't do anything to us. They want a safe house. They want somewhere quiet where people will shut up about having seen them. Well, we know to shut up. Our last year has been about shutting up. We tell anyone about our parents, and boom, they hate us. Shutting up is what we Johnsons are good at."

"I'm glad to hear that," a booming voice from the door said. "After all, we wouldn't want anyone hearing about this."

Dorian Darkmatter had arrived.

# 12

## ETHAN
### GEO

I wanted to believe that everything was going to be fine. Steven and half the Thugs had failed in a fight against me, and it was clear now that the other half would take my side over Steven's. Maybe my family didn't need to run away. Still, I didn't know what had happened to Mike, and if Steven had found Mike he would have mentioned something. I went back to the house, maybe there would be some clue in Mike's stuff. I arrived at the house and raced through the front door. Only to have a sword placed against my throat.

"Who do we have here?" the man asked, though I could not say for certain who he was.

I looked around the room. Zach was here. This could not end well. Not when it looked like he had a new gang with him.

I looked at his friends, and held back a gasp. Dorian Darkmatter. Things had just gone from bad to absolute nightmare if Dorian Darkmatter was here.

I saw Mike in the room. I breathed a sigh of relief at finding him before it clicked in my brain that he and I were both hostages.

"Mike, are you okay?" I blurted out before realizing what I'd said.

"He will be fine; Ethan, isn't it?" Dorian said to me. "I hope you do not mind that my colleagues and I have made ourselves at home in your humble abode."

I tried to remain calm, cordial. After years of knowing about my parents and dealing with supervillains, I knew how to act like I was okay with them.

"Not at all. Zach is practically family," I said.

"Good, good," Dorian said.

The blade was removed from my throat and I was encouraged to take a seat.

"You know," Dorian began, "considering your parents, I was expecting to be dealing with a family of hotheads. You and your brother are surprisingly cooperative."

I chuckled. "If you think that insulting my parents will get to me, then you don't really know me at all."

Dorian became curious at that. "You hate your parents? For being villains? So do you hate all of us too then?"

"No..." I said, "you can be a criminal, you can lie, steal, cheat, sell drugs, claw your way to the top, whatever. But beating your kids is something else."

Dorian laughed. "You are wise beyond your years, Ethan."

The teenage girl with Dorian said to me, "Where is the computer in this place?"

I felt a bit concerned as I said, "We don't have one."

"You...what?" the girl asked, stunned. I had no idea what she was capable of, but I was afraid I was about to find out.

"I'm a nineteen-year-old trying to support six kids still in school. We barely make enough for food."

She looked downright stunned, and perhaps a little bit disgusted at the thought that I didn't even have a computer.

"Poor little baby, helpless without her precious electronics," the elderly woman cackled.

"Oh shut up," the teenager snapped.

Dorian's team had the same problem that caused him to lose a year ago with the Villains Coalition. Villains struggle to work together. But whether I would be able to use it to my advantage, I didn't know.

"So...how long will you be staying with us?" I asked, trying to act like a cordial host instead of a hostage. If I seemed okay with what was happening I would be able to salvage this situation better. "We don't exactly have any guest beds, and only three of our beds are big enough for a full grown adult."

Dorian sipped the cup of coffee he had. "You are trying very hard to be civil. I appreciate it. It is far better than the cliché 'you'll never get away with this.'"

"I will have to take your word for that," I said.

"I need a computer!" the teenage girl cut in.

"You have gone without one for several months," Dorian said a bit impatiently, "you can wait several more days."

"We can't find out what people are saying without one, or at least a phone of some kind. Do you have that, at least?"

I thought about the burner phone in my pocket. I wasn't sure if I should let her know. I would need it to call James and Melissa for help.

But, James and Melissa had a baby now. I was not going to ask them to put their lives at risk.

The phone wasn't going to do anything useful for me, so I pulled it out of my pocket and handed it to the girl. "Here you are, Miss...."

"Oh, if you don't know my name there is no way I'm giving it to you. Nice try though, muscles," the girl said with a wink as she grabbed the phone.

In a couple of clicks she found what she wanted. "Okay, here's the latest. The Hero Society is calling in every hero they can from around the world in order to try and reel in all of the escaped villains. There were one thousand two hundred and thirty-seven escaped villains from the building. Fifty-eight have already been recaptured. And...oh my god, we are so screwed."

"What?" Dorian asked. "What is it?"

"For the second time in world history, the Hero Society has repealed their no-kills policy. Any villain who does not willingly surrender, and any human who aids a villain, may be killed without punishment."

All eyes fell to me after that, all of them wondering the exact same thing. If I could get killed for helping them, would I try to stop them?

# 13

## XAPHAN

The mechanical behemoth known as a car was not made with my species in mind. My wings could not adjust to a comfortable position, and after the injuries I had already sustained to them, trying to cramp them into this vehicle was painful. But I could endure it. The injuries would heal themselves in time.

"You're an interesting human," M5 said, "helping both of us out like this."

"Well, I know that being wanted by the Hero Society doesn't mean that you're a bad person. I'm gonna take the two of you to my place. My younger siblings should be okay where they are."

"Oh? What makes you say that?" M5 asked.

"Paragon herself showed up and is guarding the building where all of the children have been taken to for safe keeping. If she can't keep them safe, I don't know who can."

I did not know what they were talking about. Earth was a far more complicated place than I had expected. Far more complicated than the Underworld.

"What is the Hero Society?" I asked.

"You really don't know?" M5 asked, surprised.

"Not at all," I confessed.

"Okay," M5 said, pausing for a moment, as though deep in thought. "Recent Earth history 101: Fifteen years ago there was an alien invasion, the Earth was going to be destroyed. A different alien, named Paragon, saved us. As a last move before retreating, the aliens hit the Earth with a weapon that should have killed everyone. It didn't. Instead, some humans got superpowers. Since most people with powers go bad, the world needed powered people who do good. That's why the Hero Society was invented. They're a group of superheroes who guard the world from villains. The problem is that they consider anyone with powers who doesn't work for them to be a villain."

"So, this Hero Society, they are a singular power, controlling the world?"

"No, but they are certainly the strongest, so people hesitate to mess with them."

"We're here," Julie said as she pulled the car into the driveway.

And then Julie screamed.

I opened the door and surged out of the car. There was a young man at the door, a sword pressed against his throat by an older man.

"You will not harm the boy," I commanded as I touched the gem upon my chest.

"So, Weaponize, we meet again," M5 said as he stepped out of the car.

I could see the man holding the sword appear visibly shaken as he pulled the boy in a step.

"D-don't move, or I kill him," Weaponize said.

A man stepped out of the house and into the garage with us. His attire seemed the closest to my own of anyone I had seen.

"I should dismantle you into scrap metal for harming one of my allies," the well-attired man said, addressing M5.

"And I should slice your head off for hurting my brothers," M5 replied, "so I suppose we're even."

"Your..." the man paused, "how quaint, you view the other robots made in your image as your siblings. And you bring an angel with you. You will surrender, or I will kill this boy."

Julie stepped out of the car at that moment and begged, with tears in her eyes, "Please, do as he says. That's my brother."

My hand was stayed. I would not harm these humans M5 disliked if they were threatening someone that Julie cared about.

M5 stayed his hand as well, a quick glance over as he looked at Julie and said, "Your brother?"

"Please," Julie said, "Don't hurt Mike."

The human said, "Surrender your weapons, and come inside. Turn off the machine."

M5's hand was no longer stayed, his weapon was out and active, the energy in it converted into a gun, which he was pointing at Dorian.

"No turning me off. No touching my systems," M5 said, "anything else, fine."

"You are not in a position to negotiate," Dorian replied, "the boy will die if you don't comply."

"Then he dies," M5 replied.

"I'm surprised. I would have thought the Hero Society would make you value human life."

"My highest priority is my own survival."

I looked at M5 and said, "M5, do not presume you could defeat me. Disarm, that is your safest path."

M5 hesitated, but he did sacrifice his weapon.

Dorian smiled as he said, "I suppose it will have to do. Even without weapons the two of you are threats. You will have to remain here and be quiet until I decide it is safe to leave."

M5, Julie, and I walked into the home.  Less than a day on Earth and I had already become a prisoner again.

# 14

## MIKE
### MAGIX

"Julie!" Ethan shouted as she entered the room alongside the angel and robot.

Julie looked at Ethan and said, out loud so everyone could hear, "I took the other kids to a shelter in the centre of town. There are a dozen heroes guarding it, including Paragon."

"In light of this," Ethan said, "that was a good call."

The old woman in the corner was furiously yanking at the book in her hands.

"Open, you infuriating book. I am your new master, and you will open for me!"

The book in her hands looked really fancy, like a leather cover, but dyed to be a deep, dark purple. Not quite black, it was still easy to tell it was purple. And it had this gold square-like trim an inch in from every edge, with a bright ruby gem in the centre of it.

I couldn't see any words, and the book didn't have a latch of any kind, so there was no reason why the book wouldn't open. But it wouldn't.

"Settle down," Valerie said, "it's just a book, you old crone."

"This is not just some book, you vapid degenerate. This is the Book of Darkness!"

Curiosity killed the cat, but I just couldn't resist asking.

"What's the Book of Darkness?"

The old woman glowered at me for a moment before boasting, "Ignorant child, the Book of Darkness is the most powerful magical artifact in the entire world. The wielder of the book will have access to magic that, if used in competent hands and a brilliant mind such as my own, will make them the most powerful being on the entire planet. I will confess that adding its power to my own would be more of a lateral move in comparison to everyone else on the planet, but no one will be able to defy me once its power becomes mine." She shrieked, as the book itself blasted her and shot out of her hands.

"Looks like the book doesn't want to be wielded by you," Valerie said.

"Silence," the old woman said as she walked towards the book.

The book had fallen near me, so I moved to pick it up.

"Don't you dare touch that book, child!" the old woman shouted at me.

"Mike, just leave it be," Ethan said.

But I couldn't help myself. I needed to touch the book, for some reason.

When I touched the book, something weird happened.

The room around me disappeared. I don't know if I had moved, or if this all was in my head or something, but I was in a completely dark place, with the darkness itself swirling around me, a dull hollow wind the only sound. It felt like the darkness was crawling across my skin like a thousand bugs all over me. And the smell was so weird. It smelled kind of damp but like the smell itself made you think of your worst nightmares. It felt like my entire world had been replaced by nothing but shadows. To say I was terrified was an understatement. I couldn't see anything but darkness.

As I turned around, I noticed a figure in the darkness. I couldn't make it out very well, but it was wearing some kind of robe that seemed to be made of the very shadows all around us. As it spoke, I saw its mouth filled with razor sharp teeth. "A young boy. With a pure spirit and heart. Mmm, now you will be a good host to my power." The voice was creepy. Distinctly female, but like...gobliny or witch-like. Kind of like how the Wicked

Witch sounded in the Wizard of Oz, but more crackly and sinister sounding.

"A host?" I asked nervously. "You can give me power?"

"Yessss," it said, carrying the 's' far longer than it needed to.

"Why didn't you choose the woman?" I asked. "She wanted your power."

"She wished to control me. I cannot be controlled. I thought of letting her have access to my power, only to show her that I was controlling her, not the other way around. But I saw into her mind when she touched me. She is boring. It would be more entertaining to choose the person in the room she believes is least suited to my power. Besides, you are so delightfully sweet. I would happily bestow my power upon you."

I shuddered at her voice while liking her words. The book had chosen me. I was going to get all of the power it had. But at what cost? I wondered if this was how people felt when making a deal with the devil.

A deal with the devil would be wrong, I convinced myself. I should deny the power of the book. These shadows, the book literally being called 'of darkness' could not be good signs. But there was something more important than whether or not I made a deal with the devil.

"Can I save my brother and sister?" I asked.

"Patience, dear child, I can't give you all of my secrets in an instant," the voice said, "but rest assured, you will survive the day's events. I won't let anything happen to my precious little boy."

"Who are you?"

"Names are not important, dear child. I am sending you back. You will not speak of me."

As I returned to the world, not a moment had passed from when I had grabbed the book. But as I did, the gem on it glowed, and the book itself opened and the pages of it flipped through, opening to a page in the middle of the book.

The old woman was stunned, as was everyone else in the room. But she was the first to react.

"The book is mine, child. Hand it over."

*Tell her no*, the gobliny female voice whispered in my ear.

W*hy?* I thought at the gobliny voice.

*Because it will amuse me, dear child. I will protect you and your siblings if you do as I say. And I am not a goblin. How rude.*

I looked at the old woman and, gulping back my fear, said, "No."

The woman was outraged, her hands began to glow as magic surrounded them.

*Now, say to her, 'I have the book's power, suck it up, you old hag, you're not the strongest person in the room anymore.'*

I was terrified. This woman could kill me. But the book, I could feel its power. I knew, somehow, that the old woman couldn't hurt me.

"I have the book's power, suck it up, you old hag, you're not the strongest person in the room anymore."

The robot laughed.

The old woman shot a blast of energy that smashed a picture over the fireplace. "Old hag? You dare think you can speak to me that way? That book won't save you from my wrath. I am far too powerful for that."

*Hahahaha. She is downright adorable. She's like an infant who has never stumbled and been bruised. Completely sure of her invincibility because no one has ever put her in her place. You should kill her.*

"What? No!" I shouted instead of thinking it at the voice.

Dorian Darkmatter looked at me and said, "Boy, what is going on?"

*Tell him nothing, or you will not receive my help.*

"She destroyed the only family picture we have," I lied, "she'll pay for that."

Julie and Ethan were confused for a moment, because it was not a family picture that was destroyed.

Dorian Darkmatter stood up and declared, "We should leave. I knew the former owner of the book. I don't want to find out how much of his power the boy already has."

"I'm not leaving without MY book!" the old hag shouted.

*I see that I now have even you thinking of her as a hag.*

*You're not helping,* I thought at the voice.

"Where would we go?" Valerie said. "You have a dozen safe houses and yet we chose here instead. Because we need somewhere to lay low that they wouldn't think to check."

"This isn't up for debate," Dorian replied angrily. "We leave, or we kill the boy."

The tension in the room was undeniable. It felt like time froze for a moment as everyone was trying to decide whether to fight or run.

It was at that moment that a window of the house burst open, and a flash-bang grenade went off.

I should have been deafened or silenced by it. But I was oddly unaffected.

*One of my many gifts, dear child. Such mundane devices shall not affect your perception.*

Jumping through the window shortly after was a person in an almost solid grey outfit, with some patches of brown on it, along with a brown cape and cowl.

*A brave girl, to enter a place of such power with nothing but her own skill at arms. And at such a young age as well.*

"Dorian Darkmatter," the masked girl shouted, "you're under arrest!"

# 15

## M5

My sensors were blinded briefly as the grenade went off.

But I recovered from it faster than most, and witnessed a girl in a brown and grey outfit attacking Dorian Darkmatter.

I scanned her height, build, and skill, and did a search of known heroes while also activating the handaptable and turning it into a sword. One of the first search results to come up that fit was about Claire O'Sheen, a sidekick named Osprey who had her secret identity revealed to the world earlier that day. And she had been banned from being a sidekick or hero because of it. There was no doubt that this was her in a different costume.

Breaking her superhero ban within hours of receiving it, it didn't take me long to decide I liked her.

"Xaphan, let's help her out," I said as I charged at the biggest threat in the room, Monster.

I sliced at Monster again, my blows barely scratching her, but definitely enough to grab her attention.

I twisted my head to see what was going on around me, only to get clocked in the head and sent flying into a wall. I really needed to restore my vision. I couldn't afford to take my eyes off my opponent in the middle of a fight, that was stupid.

Monster certainly was feeling vengeful and tore a couch in two as she raced at me.

That was when Xaphan got in the way and a burst of red/black flames shot out of their fist at Monster. The flames hit Monster square in the chest and Monster screamed in pain. I could actually see searing and scarring from the wound.

"How did..." I asked Xaphan as I jumped to my feet and readied to deal with the next threat.

"Hellfire is one of the most powerful substances in creation," Xaphan replied. "Nothing is immune to it."

"Okay, how about you handle that one then," I said.

Before Xaphan could respond, I sped over and swung at Weaponize, who pulled out his pair of swords and blocked the blow.

I changed the handaptable into a whip, wrapped it around Weaponize's neck and yanked him to the ground.

A quick glance to my right showed me that the teenage boy had some power of his own, and was fighting against Dorian Darkmatter alongside the hero girl. Book kid was standing around, terrified, not that I could blame him.

I removed the whip from Weaponize and converted it to a gun, which I used to shoot him in the chest. The blow didn't break through Weaponize's armour though.

The hero girl shouted at me, "Attack Dorian!"

"I'm busy!" I shouted back as Weaponize drew his assault pistols and fired at me.

The girl backflipped away from Dorian and almost kicked the boy with the book.

But I was a little busy with my own problem, and more.

Monster had managed to grab Xaphan and was crushing the life out of her. I evaded Weaponize's shots as I charged at Monster, only for Xaphan to show me why I didn't need to.

Xaphan's fists erupted with dark flames and Monster let go, her skin charred by the flames.

Monster was not used to feeling pain of that level. And with a broken wall left in her wake, Monster burst out of the house and ran away.

"Get back here, you coward!" Dorian shouted at Monster as she left.

With one threat out of the way, I didn't feel as bad focusing on my problem. Weaponize was ready for me, a sword in one hand, a gun in the other. He fired at me, and I turned the handaptable into a shield fast enough to deflect the blow. I transformed it back into a sword and charged at him.

He blocked with his sword, and was about to shoot into my chest when I punched him in the stomach. The blow winded him. And I took advantage of it to hit him in the face.

He staggered away from the blow and moved towards Mother Time.

I charged at him as I realized that Mother Time was in a trance. I searched through my files to find out what that trance could mean. And came up with nothing. Magic was just too weird, no one could predict it.

But then, Mother Time's eyes glowed red for a brief moment, and I knew that something bad was going to happen.

Appearing out of thin air, like they had been teleported in, were a dozen of what could only be described as demons. Boney demons. Their red flesh clung to their bones so tightly it was hard to believe they weren't just skeletons until you noticed the tail and wings, or the talons at the end of their arms. Plus, they were all at least seven feet tall.

I shuddered as I realized that no one had been trying to stop Mother Time, and that this was clearly the price to pay for ignoring the person who knows magic.

I swung my blade at one of the demons. Its arm came up to block it. Although I could see some black ichor that could be mistaken for its blood oozing out, my blow barely scrapped it. I was right to think they were boney, and their bones were tougher than my weapon could penetrate.

"Gonna need some help," I shouted, right before one of them slashed down my chest with its claws.

Those claws were sharper than I would have expected. They ripped my chest plate of armour to shreds. A couple sparks flew out of me and I tried to bolt away from them only for one of the demons to grab my already damaged leg. He was about to toss me into a wall when I kicked up and gave him a face full of flames from my still functioning rocket boot.

The demon screamed in agony and clutched at its face, letting go of me just long enough for me to bolt out of the way and switch to fighting back from a distance, the handaptable converting to a gun in my hand as I aimed for the face of another one.

Ethan seemed ready to help now that he could see outside. A boulder of earth came hurling through the ground behind Mother Time, but one of the demons punched the dirt and it splintered and shattered from the impact.

With her creations now around, Mother Time was starting to get into the fight herself. I saw her fire a blast of magic towards the boy with the book.

Without even thinking about it, I leapt in the way of the attack. Magic isn't supposed to work on machines, so I hoped that my newfound sentience wouldn't make me an exception to the rule.

The blast hit me square in the chest, and did absolutely nothing to me. If I breathed I would have sighed with relief right then, but instead I just focused on the room and where I was needed.

Ethan was trying to distract the demons with a bunch of dirt and earth and rock, but it wasn't going to be enough.

Xaphan had begun taking the fight to the demons. Her flames burst at one of them, burning a hole through its chest. But Mother Time fired a blast of green energy at the demon, and the hole in its chest repaired itself, the demon back on its feet almost instantly.

I fired a few shots from my gun at Mother Time, but the blasts were all blocked by the demons, able to react to my shots fast enough to intercept them before they hit Mother Time.

I turned the handaptable into a sword and rushed back into the fight, even though I was injured.

These things were protecting Mother Time, and this fight wouldn't be over until she was dealt with. A quick glance showed me that Xaphan and I might be on our own to fight these demons; Claire, Ethan, and Zach were all occupied dealing with Dorian Darkmatter.

I almost regretted saving Xaphan in that moment. Almost. I would still do it again. Still save Xaphan, still be here to fight them all. I may want to live, but not if someone else has to die.

I slashed at the eyes of one of the demons and slid underneath him as I raced towards Mother Time. The fight wouldn't be over until she and Dorian were down and out.

# 16

## VALERIE
### STELLAR

There were demons in the living room. Demons! I shouldn't have had to deal with that. No one should have to live in a world where people could make demons appear out of thin air. It was ridiculous. I needed a way out.

"Dorian," I shouted, "we need to get out of here!"

"These heroes took a year of my life. They're going to pay."

"Stop thinking about revenge and open a portal," I shouted at him.

He ignored me. Well I wasn't going to wait around and get killed, hurt, or caught because of him. I raced for the unprotected back door. I was getting out of there alive and free.

I ran out the door, and found myself back in the living room, in the middle of the fight. I looked behind me quickly and saw a Dorian portal.

Dorian pushed me to the ground with his powers, increasing gravity on me. Making me so heavy that I...I couldn't move.

I couldn't even speak, the pressure on my vocal cords was too much.

Under the pressure, the little Petri dish in my pocket cracked and the last of my nanites came out.

I felt them moving along my body. Which shouldn't have been possible. But I then realized that I wasn't feeling them on my skin. I was feeling my skin through them.

I'd practiced a mental link for the nanites back before they took my research away from me, but it had never worked all that well before. I wasn't going to complain though. I needed every possible advantage I could get, even if it didn't make sense.

I thought about the nanites combining, and using the solar energy they had stored within them to fire a laser at Dorian Darkmatter.

And it worked. A small, bullet-like laser, shot into the air, and hit Dorian in the stomach. I could see some blood coming from the wound.

His focus was gone, and I jumped to my feet. The nanites were on the back of my right hand. I commanded ten of the nanites to leave me, to find more metal and convert it into further nanites. They knew how to replicate. They would do as I commanded. I just wasn't sure if they could do it fast enough. Or if I could survive very long with what I had.

Because all I had was a tiny laser on my wrist. And there was no way that was going to save me against everyone in here. I needed to get out.

But I was caught in the middle of it all. A half dozen of these heroes, villains, and monsters in my way in every single direction. The only way out was to fight.

The boy with the book looked at me. "I thought you worked for Dorian."

"I just want out of here," I answered.

"Help us?" he asked me.

I hesitated. What had any of them ever done for me? I barely even knew them. They weren't worth risking my life over.

I shouldn't have spent so much time thinking in the middle of a battle. A demon grabbed me in one of its enormous hands and slammed me into the ground. I felt one of my ribs crack. I thought about the nanites, and commanded them to move into my chest and fix my broken rib. That kind of repair work was what they were originally designed for.

But it wouldn't be enough until I could get out of the demon's grip.

The angel helped me with that, to my surprise.

A stream of fire mixed with black shot out of its fist, like fire and shadow mixed together.

The demon released me, and I stumbled towards the door. I didn't care that the angel had saved me. I didn't owe those people anything. I just wanted to run out the door and get as far away as possible. Maybe find a lab, or do my research on my own. No more heroes, no more villains, just my science.

That was when another one of the demons grabbed me, and tossed me through a wall.

My head was spinning. I touched the top of my head and there was blood. I was lucid enough to realize that I had a concussion. It was getting harder to stay awake. Harder to focus. But focus I had to. I needed to live. And I needed my nanites to do that for me.

The nanites returned to me, a small swarm of them, moving through the room, coming at me from the kitchen.

But the conversion took a lot more time than that. There was a small amount, a couple spoonful's, but that was it.

The nanites came to my body, some going inward to help fix the cracked rib. The remainder went to my head, trying to fix the bleeding and the brain injury.

I felt them tapping into my brain, felt the nanites saving me, fixing me.

I stood up as the nanites formed a gun-like structure on my wrist. I thought about shooting Dorian and a laser shot out of the gun that hit Dorian and knocked him back into the wall.

Dorian looked at me, scared. He was huffing and puffing, and his clothing was singed from the blast. "You can't win," he ground out.

"Maybe," I replied, "but I can take you down with me."

I pulled my left arm up, a gun-like structure on its wrist too now, and I fired both guns at Dorian.

The shots missed, but Dorian was scared now, and was ready to get out. I saw one of his portals open up and he disappeared, taking Weaponize with him.

All that was left was Mother Time. And a dozen demons. I still didn't like my odds.

# 17

## MIKE
### MAGIX

Dorian was gone, but that wasn't going to be enough when Mother Time had summoned so many demons, or monsters, or whatever they were.

The hero girl and the tech girl were fighting one of the demons, and Ethan and Uncle Zach were holding off a couple more. The angel was taking on a couple itself, and the robot was hopping around everywhere it could to stop the demons from hurting anyone. But no one could get at Mother Time. The demons were protecting her too well. There had to be something I could do.

*There is, dear child,* the gobliny voice said.

*How?* I thought.

*Your magic is powerful. More than this insipid witch shall ever possess. But if you wish it to work, you must learn how to focus. Distractions, such as concern for the safety of your brother and sister, will only get in the way of your magic functioning properly. Focus on exactly what the magic should do, without concern for anything else.*

I was trying to focus, but then one of the demons got past Ethan, it was coming straight at me. Ethan, Zach, and the robot all moved to intercept. But all of them failed.

I stood there, terrified. I tried to duck, but the demon struck at me with its claws.

The attack bounced off, and the demonic skeleton shot back and straight through the wall, an energy barrier protecting me from the attack.

*Hehehe. As if the magic of such an amateur could ever harm my chosen one.*

Mother Time was surprised. And furious.

"Your magic is nothing compared to the book," I shouted at her.

I charged at the monsters, and I punched at one. It did nothing. The demon was not hurt. It swatted me to the side and I flew through the wall. Unhurt.

*What happened?* I thought at the voice.

*I'm not going to protect you if you continue to behave stupidly. You have magic. Why would you try and punch them?*

That took a moment to think about. I wasn't too sure how to fight without punching. Until I saw Uncle Zach shoot one of the demons with the energy from his hands. I thought about creating energy in my hands. I focused on that, and my hands began to glow with energy. I shot the energy at the demonic skeleton, and it went flying through the wall.

The house started to shake.

We had put too many holes in the building, the roof was starting to collapse on us.

I had to focus. The roof needed to stay up. I could feel the roof above me, I could see a faint purple glow to it. It had stopped shaking; it was not going to fall on us. Now there were just the monsters to deal with.

The roof started to fall again, and my focus returned to keeping it off of the group.

*Throw it.* The voice said to me. *You must learn to get rid of one thing so that you can focus on the next; move the roof.*

I focused. I thought about the top floor of the house, about the roof. And I thought about moving it. It was slow going, yet it didn't feel heavy. I was moving it with my magic. The hard part was focusing on it with all of the noise and distractions going on around me. But focus I did. I moved the upper floor of the house and gently placed it into the backyard.

The others were in trouble. I could see the tech girl getting squeezed by another one of the monsters, and my brother wasn't doing so hot either.

Then one of them found Julie in her hiding spot and grabbed her.

"Save her!" the costumed girl shouted at the robot.

"I don't take orders from humans!" the robot responded.

"Please, save my sister," I shouted.

The robot was pretty quick to respond to that, and after a quick slash, the monster let go of my sister.

The angel looked over at the costumed girl. "These beasts do not fall."

"We have to attack her," the girl said, pointing at Mother Time, "if we attack her, the monsters will go away."

*Clever girl,* the voice said to me.

*She's right then?*

*For someone with the limited power of a normal human, her plan is a good one. Of course, we have better options.*

I shot a blast of magic at one of the monsters, pushing it away from Uncle Zach as he shot another one.

*I'm open to suggestions,* I said to the voice in my head.

*Now now, how's my dear child supposed to learn if I simply give him the answer?*

I had to think. What could I do? I shot another blast at one of the monsters, wishing I could find a way to get at Mother Time.

*You have the strongest magic in the world at your fingertips and all you can think to do is shoot them?*

There was a better way to deal with the problem, I just needed to figure out what it was, because the voice in my head already knew.

*Oh, child, would you like a hint? I may give you one if you'll do something for me.*

I wasn't too sure about that. The voice did not feel trustworthy. But I needed to save my brother and sister and everyone else.

*Fine, deal. Just help me save everyone*, I thought at the voice.

*It's really quite simple*, the voice began. *How did those monsters appear?*

*She created them*, I replied mentally.

*She created them with magic.*

*So?* I demanded.

*Your magic is stronger. Unmake them.*

I was dumbfounded. It couldn't be that simple, but I had to try.

I began to focus. Focus on making them go away.

I felt a tug of resistance against my attempts. Mother Time's magic was opposing mine. I could feel her strength, her power. Her power was tremendous.

*Her power is nothing, dear boy. You simply lack experience.*

"BEGONE!" I shouted, my focus manifesting into words.

My hands glowed a pale purple as each of the monsters was surrounded by the same colour. They all paused for a second.

The others saw that for the opportunity it was. Uncle Zach sent a blast of energy at one right in its head so strong that it exploded. Ethan rammed a boulder into another. The angel's fire burned a hole through one of them. But that was all before they began moving again.

I was trying to do too much all at once. I focused on one demon. Just one, who was protecting Mother Time. It screamed in agony as it dissolved.

The hero girl saw the opening and raced at Mother Time, only to be blocked by another demon. I focused my attention on that one as it grasped the hero girl and tried to crush her in its arms. And it disappeared too.

"Surrender or leave," I said to Mother Time as I looked over at another demon and made it vanish.

A puff of smoke appeared around Mother Time, and she disappeared, along with the few remaining demons she had.

We won.

# 18

## CLAIRE
### THE SPARROW

Mother Time was dealt with. The fight was almost won, and all because these villains had been fighting each other. I charged at Blaster immediately, he was the most experienced threat in the group.

That was when almost all of them got in my way. I stopped in my tracks when I saw none of them trying to pull a punch.

"What are you doing?" the android practically shouted at me, its weapon deactivated.

"I know what you are," I said to the android, "does your creator know you're here?"

"No, I don't answer to him anymore," the android replied, "I'm M5. Thanks for the help."

I could feel all of their eyes on me. When I started the last fight, I'd had the element of surprise. But right now, right now I was in the middle of a group of villains. I'd made it out of worse before. Heck, I'd made it out of worse that morning.

"We don't want to fight," Geo said, looking at me.

"Like I can believe a word any of you say," I shouted as I spun around, trying to make sure none of them struck me from behind. They had me surrounded.

"You helped me save my brother and sister," Geo said, "I want to thank you, not fight you."

"You're one of the Thugs, and so is he," I said as I pointed at Blaster.

"He never wanted to be a Thug," Blaster began, "I just wanted him to be. I talked him into it 'cause he needed the money to support his siblings. And, yet, look at this house. No TV, no computer, no phones. The guy was robbing banks for me and he refused to take more than the bare minimum to get by because he's too wracked with guilt."

"Ethan, is that...is that true?" the boy with the book asked.

"Yeah, Mike...yeah, it is."

I could see the look of disappointment on Mike's face, and the look of guilt on Geo's...no, Ethan's. He had been blackmailed into being a villain.

"Well, this is all just peachy, but I'm gonna go before Little Miss Righteous decides to try and fight us again," the dark-skinned girl said as she turned to leave. I think her name was Valerie, now that I had a chance for a good look at her, but I wasn't sure. I didn't remember the names of all the villains the Hero Society had locked away.

I tossed a throwing star in her direction. She turned around with a wrist-mounted gun aimed at me. "I said, I'm leaving," she replied.

I looked her dead in the eyes, "You're wanted by the Hero Society, I'm taking you in. All of you."

"And yourself along with us," M5 said.

I glared at him as he took a step closer to me.

"What are you talking about?"

"I know who you are, Claire O'Sheen," M5 replied. "And I know that you were banned from heroing by the Society earlier today. It doesn't matter if you could bring us all in. They'll arrest you too for breaking your ban. You should be on our side, we're all in the same boat here."

My fists shook with anger as the android stared me down. He couldn't possibly be right. I had been a good sidekick for six years. I may have screwed up, but once I proved how valuable I was, they would let me back in. I was sure of it. They'd let people back in before.

"You're not going to be an exception, Claire," M5 said to me, "they won't care that your mother is The Eagle."

He was trying to trick me. Trying to talk me down. It was all a lie. I knew that.

But I couldn't help thinking that he wasn't actually wrong. I'd seen it before. I'd seen spurned lovers of superheroes try and reveal secret identities only to be locked away. I'd seen heroes who screwed up get arrested. But I knew they wouldn't do that to me.

"If you think I'm just going to...to...stand aside and let a group of criminals roam free, or let the boy keep that book...."

The boy walked over to me and held out the book. "Take it. It's too dangerous. The Hero Society should have it."

It felt like some kind of trick. But the boy had helped me. So I grabbed the book from him.

And I think it almost killed him. His eyes went wide, and his mouth shot wide open. He was gasping for breath, choking to death.

I didn't wait for permission from his brother or sister. I grabbed him in my arms and started performing the Heimlich maneuver, but it wasn't doing anything. I could see his breathing becoming worse, could see his face turning purple from lack of oxygen. I laid him down on the ground, trying to look into his mouth to see if I could see anything.

"You," I shouted at Valerie, "You fixed yourself in the fight, can you fix him?"

"Yeah, my nanites should be able to," she said as she came in. I could see the gun on her left wrist disintegrate as the nanites moved into the boy's body.

After a couple of seconds, the boy's face was even more purple, and the nanites hadn't accomplished anything.

"They're...they're not working," the girl said, "something is stopping them."

"The book," M5 replied, "give him back the book!"

I didn't hesitate. I grabbed the book and shoved it into the boy's hands. The purple disappeared from his face instantly. He didn't even take a huge gasp of air. He was fine, like it had never happened. Like he hadn't been seconds away from dying.

"What just happened?" the angel asked.

"It's the book," M5 explained, "I looked up everything I could on its former owners. They died if the book was taken from them, or they tried to give it away."

I stood up. I was grateful for my mask; it hid the tears in my eyes. I couldn't do it. Even if that book was one of the most powerful items of evil in the world, I couldn't take it if it would kill the boy. He'd done nothing wrong. Just had the bad luck to pick up a book of pure evil. Even if I brought him to the Society, they'd lock him up for having the book. But he had used the book to help us. Maybe...maybe the book wasn't bad, it was just those who wielded it.

"I guess...I guess he can keep the book," I said.

"And the rest of us?" the tech girl asked.

"You're a criminal," I said.

"My crime was performing research into nanotechnology. My crime was using my tech to create weapons that would let anyone have the same power as a superhero. Let militaries and police have the weapons they need to fight supervillains if there aren't any heroes around."

I paused as I looked at her. A quiet, stunned voice that barely resembled mine squeaked out, "That's it?"

"That's it," she said firmly, "your precious Hero Society had me in jail for three months over that. I just tried to get my tech back."

"And you," I said, looking over at the angel, "the fire you used doesn't look like any I've seen before. Remiel told me enough for me to guess that you're a Fallen angel."

"I am," the angel said, his...or was it her...face completely stoic. There was no challenge to her tone.

"Fallen angels serve Lucifer, that makes them evil."

"My only crime was trying to stop the war between Lucifer and those still residing in the Upper

Planes thousands of years ago. By not siding against Lucifer, I was assumed to have sided with Lucifer."

"Besides," M5 interrupted, "Xaphan hasn't committed any crimes on Earth. It's just Remiel using his status in the Hero Society to arrest someone he doesn't like."

I looked at M5. "And what of you?"

"I'm sentient now. I can think and make decisions for myself. My creator wanted to examine that, even at the risk of me losing my sentience. If I were a human, that would be illegal, so it should be illegal to do it to me too."

I looked at all of them with new eyes now. A man forced into crime, a girl with advanced tech who was trying to use it to defend the world better, the first sentient robot defending his right to live, a boy whose life depended on a supposedly evil book, and an angel lumped in with evil for trying to stop a war. None of them were truly villains.

I looked at Ethan, pointed directly at him, and said, "You're done. No more working with the Thugs."

"That's not a problem," Ethan replied.

"So, what now?" Julie asked.

"You know," M5 said, "There are a lot of villains out there now. And we make a pretty good team."

I almost laughed at the idea. To think that the six of us could become a team was hysterical. "Right, a bunch of wanted criminals becoming heroes."

"We defeated a team of villains that included Dorian Darkmatter, Mother Time, and Monster. All three of them are in the top ten most powerful supervillains of all time."

He was right. But I knew it couldn't work out. Heroes working without the Society's approval would never work. And every single one of them was wanted by the Hero Society. Targets would be on their backs from day one.

"You'll be hunted," I said.

M5 looked at me, and then at the others, as he said, "We're going to be hunted one way or another by the very people who claim to be heroes. We may as well have each other's backs while we do it. And maybe try and do the right thing along the way. Stop criminals, save people. We have the power to help, I'm not going to squander it just because I want to keep myself safe, or because I'm not willing to follow someone else's rules for how I'm supposed to go about helping."

Mike spoke up, looking at the book in his hands with both excitement and concern. "If...if I can figure out how this book works, if I can use it for good, just think of everything I could do to help people."

"Mike," Ethan said, "no, I don't want you getting hurt."

"But M5 is right, Ethan. If we can help people, we need to. Julie and I are safe right now because they all helped us. Could you let someone else lose their little brother or sister when you could have helped?"

I read Ethan's lips as he whispered to himself, "Dang it, Mike" before responding aloud, "No, I couldn't."

"I'm in too," Valerie said.

"You want to be a hero? You were working with Dorian Darkmatter."

"I just wanted my tech back, and some muscle to help keep me safe. If I'm going to be hunted anyways, best to have someone watching my back."

"What about you, Xaphan?" M5 asked.

Xaphan hesitated. "I was sent to observe. Not interfere. But it seems that is not an option for me. I will join."

"How about you, Claire?"

"Sparrow," I replied, "my new name is Sparrow."

"Alright, Sparrow, you in?"

I wasn't sure. And that startled me. I couldn't believe that I was actually considering working with them. "I don't know."

I looked around at what had happened. At the house destroyed around us. I think my thoughts drifted a bit, because my next comment was, "This house is too far gone. There are going to be questions. Lots of them. And if they find out Dorian was here, there won't be an end to the questions asked."

"So they don't find out," Blaster replied.

I wasn't the only set of eyes that turned to Blaster after that comment.

"Arrest me. Blame me for the whole thing. Me attacking the Johnsons makes complete sense, no one will look that closely into it. That way, everyone else can get away. It's the least I can do for how much I've screwed up their lives. I never should have pulled Ethan into a life of crime. I can't do much to make up for it, but I can take the blame for this so that no one will ask any questions."

"Zach," Ethan began, "you don't have to do this for me. Not again."

"It's okay," Zach said, removing his control gauntlets and putting his arms out to be cuffed.

I pulled a pair of handcuffs out of my utility belt and slapped them on Blaster. They were Hero Society design, power suppressing.

I was about to walk away with Blaster when Ethan said to me, "You're sure about this, Claire? You could get arrested too."

"I'll be fine," I said to Ethan, surprised at his concern, "someone has to take him in to the Hero Society."

"Wait," M5 said.

"What?" I asked before leaving.

"We need a name," M5 responded.

Everyone looked at him, confused. "Look, there's the Thugs, the Villains Coalition, the Hero Society—we need a name too."

"How about the Rebels?" Mike suggested.

"Overused," Valerie responded, "too cliché."

"Outcasts?" Ethan suggested.

"Not bad, on the right track," M5 replied.

"Renegades," I replied as I walked away with Zach in cuffs.

I could practically here the wheels in M5's head turning as he said, "Renegade, an individual who rejects lawful or conventional behaviour...I like it."

I left the scene of the crime, Zach in handcuffs. Ready to lie about what had really happened in order to protect the rest of them. Even if I did get reinstated as a hero, I knew in that moment that I would still be a Renegade.

Born and raised in Saskatoon, Saskatchewan, Brian James Hildebrand wanted to be an author since he was ten years old—and was determined to become one before he turned twelve. Eighteen years later, he succeeded. This is Brian's second novel, created out of his love for superheroes.

CPSIA information can be obtained
at www.ICGtesting.com
Printed in the USA
FSOW04n0548150417
33115FS